Cast of D0446197

Kate Rebel: Matriarch of the Rebel family.

Falcon: The oldest son—the strong one. Abandoned by his wife, Leah, following the birth of their daughter, Eden.

Egan: The loner. Married to Rachel Hollister, daughter of the man who put him in jail.

Quincy: The peacemaker. In love with Jenny Walker, his brother's girlfriend.

Elias: The fighter. Falls in love with the daughter of their archenemy.

Paxton: The lover. Never met a woman he couldn't have, but the woman he wants doesn't want him.

Jude: The serious, responsible one. Raising his small son alone.

Phoenix: The wild one and the youngest. He's independent and free until Child Protective Services says he's the father of a small boy.

Abraham (Abe) Rebel: Paternal grandfather.

Jericho Johnson: Egan's friend from prison.

Dear Reader,

Texas Rebels: Falcon is the second book in the Texas Rebels miniseries for Harlequin American Romance. The series is loosely connected to *A Texas Holiday Miracle*, *One Night in Texas* and *The Sheriff of Horseshoe, Texas*.

As I told you in Egan's Dear Reader letter, this series came to me in a dream about seven brothers who cope in different ways with their father's death. I also dreamed their names, which was great because it's hard to come up with names to fit a character. I wasn't all that crazy about Falcon, but as I wrote his story I began to love his name. Since he's the oldest, he became the head of family after John Rebel died. Falcon has a lot of responsibility on his shoulders, running a big ranch and keeping his brothers in line. He is also the strong one so he's up for the task.

That is until his wife, Leah, who had left him and their three-month-old daughter almost eighteen years ago, returns. His strength is tested many times as he deals with his feelings about her sudden return. I have to warn you this is an emotional book. I had to stop several times and get away from the computer since I couldn't see because of the tears. Falcon and Leah are two strong-willed characters with frailties and faults, as you will see while they struggle to forgive and move on. I put them through a lot, but I was rooting for them all the way. I hope you will be, too.

With love and thanks,

Linda Warren

You can email me at Lw1508@aol.com, visit my website at lindawarren.net, send me a message on Facebook (LindaWarrenAuthor) or Twitter (@Texauthor), or write me at PO Box 5182, Bryan, TX 77805. Your mail and thoughts are deeply appreciated.

TEXAS REBELS: FALCON

LINDA WARREN

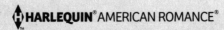

Recycling programs
for this product may
not exist in your area.

ISBN-13: 978-0-373-75578-3

Texas Rebels: Falcon

Copyright © 2015 by Linda Warren

Printed in U.S.A.

www.Harlequin.com

Two-time RITA® Award-nominated and award-winning author **Linda Warren** loves her job, writing happily-ever-after books for Harlequin. Drawing upon her years of growing up on a farm/ranch in Texas, she writes about sexy heroes, feisty heroines and broken families with an emotional punch, all set against the backdrop of Texas. Her favorite pastime is sitting on her patio with her husband watching the wildlife, especially the injured ones that are coming in pairs these days: two Canada geese with broken wings, two does with broken legs and a bobcat ready to pounce on anything tasty. Learn more about Linda and her books at her website, lindawarren.net, or on Facebook, LindaWarrenAuthor, or follow @Texauthor on Twitter.

Books by Linda Warren

Harlequin American Romance

The Christmas Cradle
"Merry Texmas" in *Christmas, Texas Style*
The Cowboy's Return
Once a Cowboy
Texas Heir
The Sheriff of Horseshoe, Texas
Her Christmas Hero
Tomas: Cowboy Homecoming
One Night in Texas
A Texas Holiday Miracle

Texas Rebels

Texas Rebels: Egan

Visit lindawarren.net for more titles.

Acknowledgments

The internet is an invaluable source
and I used it extensively to research brain tumors.
Some of the personal stories tugged at my heart.
A big thanks to the women who were
willing to share their ordeal.

A special thanks to Phyllis Phucas, RN,
for graciously sharing her knowledge and
answering my many questions about preemies.

All errors are strictly mine.

Dedication

I dedicate this book to Elaine Weldon,
a faithful reader. She loved my books and would
tell anyone who would listen about them.
I will miss her shining face at book signings.
Soar with the angels, Elaine.

Prologue

My name is Kate Rebel. I married John Rebel when I was eighteen years old and then bore him seven sons. We worked the family ranch, which John later inherited. We put everything we had into buying more land so our sons would have a legacy. We didn't have much, but we had love.

The McCray Ranch borders Rebel Ranch on the east and the McCrays have forever been a thorn in my family's side. They've cut our fences, dammed up creeks to limit our water supply and shot one of our prize bulls. Ezra McCray threatened to shoot our sons if he caught them jumping his fences again. We tried to keep our boys away, but they are boys—young and wild.

One day Jude and Phoenix, two of our youngest, were out riding together. When John heard shots, he immediately went to find his boys. They lay on the ground, blood oozing from their heads. Ezra McCray was astride a horse twenty yards away with a rifle in his hand. John drew his gun and fired, killing Ezra instantly. Both boys survived with only minor wounds. Since my husband was protecting his children, he didn't spend even one night in jail. This escalated the feud that still goes on today.

The man I knew as my husband died that day. He couldn't live with what he'd done, and started to drink heavily. I had to take over the ranch and the raising of our boys. John died ten years later. We've all been affected by the tragedy, especially my sons.

They are grown men now and deal in different ways with the pain of losing their father. One day I pray my boys will be able to put this behind them and live healthy, normal lives with women who will love them the way I loved their father.

Chapter One

Falcon: the oldest son—the strong one.

A time to forget...

Eighteen years was long enough to wait for his wife to come home. Today Falcon Rebel would stop waiting.

Every time the phone rang he tensed. Every time the news came on and someone's body had been found he could barely breathe until he heard the person's identity. Every time his daughter mentioned her name he searched his mind for reasons why Leah would leave him and their three-month-old baby.

What could possibly justify her actions? It had been a long labor and a difficult birth, and Leah was different afterward. He'd tried talking to her, but nothing worked. She had wanted to be left alone, and then one day he came home to find a note on the bed. It was simple: "I need time. Leah." No *love*. Nothing. Just like that, she was gone from their lives.

Standing on his balcony looking out over Rebel Ranch, his eyes strayed to the tall oaks in the distance shading Yaupon Creek. They'd made love there for the first time. She was a virgin and scared, and he had wanted to make it special for her. It had been, but they were just teenagers playing adults. Getting pregnant in high school wasn't in their plans. They'd gotten married, though, because it was the right thing to do. Leah moved into his room on the ranch and he was sure they could make it. They loved each other.

He sighed and ran his hands through his hair. Love didn't last long when the responsibilities of life took over, and living with family didn't help. They had no time alone except in his room. The harsh realities of life had hit them hard, but still he was sure they could make their marriage work until he saw the note. Everything ended that day and he grew up faster than he had ever imagined he would.

Raising their daughter without a mother had been the biggest challenge of his life, and then his dad had died and his world had come crashing down around him. By then he wasn't sure of anything. All he knew was he had to survive for his daughter. And he had to be strong for his mother and his brothers. The responsibility of the ranch weighed heavily upon his shoulders. He'd donned the mantle of head of the family and had never looked back.

With his eyes fixed on the tall oaks, he had to admit forgetting Leah wasn't ever going to happen. Not until he knew if she was dead or alive.

"Dad!" his daughter, Eden, shouted.

"I'm here." He stepped back into his room and closed the French doors. His beautiful seventeen-year-old, dark-haired, green-eyed daughter stood in his room with her hand over her eyes.

"Are you decent?"

"Yeah."

Eden had a habit of running in and out of his room whenever she wanted. About two months ago she caught him shaving in his underwear and it had embarrassed her. He was happy to know she had some boundaries. Leah had been a shy, timid girl, but their daughter was just the opposite.

Feisty and outgoing, Eden never met a stranger. And she had a temper that could peel the paint off the walls. Her teenage years had given him more gray hair than he had really wanted, but she was the light of his life and he couldn't imagine a day without her. Soon she would go off to college and he would have to let go. He was still grappling with that.

"Grandma wants to know why you're not down for breakfast. You're always the first one to get a cup of coffee. Are you feeling okay?" She laughed that funny little laugh of hers. "What am I asking? You're healthy as a horse." Then her eyes narrowed as if something could be wrong and she had missed it. "Aren't you?"

He put an arm around her waist. "You bet, baby girl. Let's go."

They walked down the stairs arm in arm. At the bottom Eden said, "Dad."

"No."

She stomped her foot and they came to a stop. "Why do you always do that? You don't give me a chance to say what I want to say."

He kissed the tip of her nose. "I know that tone. You want something that I'm not going to like and you make your voice all sweet and sugary."

"Can you read my mind, too?"

"Yes," he replied and walked into the kitchen. "Morning, Mom."

"Morning." Kate Rebel handed him a cup of coffee. Dressed in old jeans, boots and a long-sleeved Western shirt, she was ready for a day on the ranch.

"Mom, I can get my own coffee."

"Who said you couldn't? There's scrambled eggs, bacon and biscuits on the stove. We have a full day ahead of us."

His mom worked as hard as anyone on the ranch. Just once he would like for her to take it easy, but he knew that was out of the question. The ranch and her sons were her life.

He filled his plate and sat at the table. Eden sat across from him, munching on a biscuit.

"Dad, I want to talk to you."

He took a sip of coffee. "Okay, what is it?"

Eden scooted forward in her chair, her eyes eager. At times when he looked at her, he saw Leah. His daughter definitely favored her mother, but her personality was more like his and that's what worried him.

"I've been thinking. And don't get all frowny face until I finish."

"I don't get frowny face."

Eden rolled her eyes. "Whatever. I know you want me to go to Baylor. We visited the university and all, but I'd rather help Uncle Quincy with the paint horses. I love working with them, and why can't I work on the ranch like everyone else? Why do I have to leave?"

Because I want you to have the best of everything.

Instead of saying that, he took a moment and tried to see this from her point of view. But he hit a brick wall.

"You keep telling me how you'll be eighteen soon and an adult, free to do what you want, go out with your friends and basically have the freedom that you keep saying I deny you. Well, if you stay here on the ranch, guess who's going to be watching over you and dictating what you do and where you go?"

"Ah, Dad."

"You're going to college, Eden. That's my bottom line."

She scooted even closer, her green eyes gleaming. "But listen to what I want to do. Uncle Quincy has this amazing paint. Her name is Dancing Cloud but we call her Dancer. She's fast, Dad. Really fast. Uncle Quincy put some barrels up and I've been barrel racing her. Uncle Quincy says I'm good and that's what I want to do. I want to stay on the ranch and rodeo like Uncle Paxton and Uncle Phoenix."

Falcon took a deep breath to keep words from spewing out. He counted to ten before he spoke. "You want to rodeo?"

"Yeah, Dad. I can do it. I'm really good."

He shook his head, wondering if all parents had this much difficulty understanding their children. Why wasn't she jumping at the chance to go to college? Wasn't that every girl's dream? He had to be careful or he'd lose her in a way he hadn't even thought about.

"Why aren't you saying anything?" His daughter was impatient.

He could put his foot down and say no, but he had to listen to her ideas. She was older now and he had to learn to be lenient. Or at least try.

"School has just started, so why don't you get your rodeo card and attend some weekend rodeos to see how you like it and see how this amazing horse does before we go changing plans."

She jumped up and threw her arms around his neck. "I love you, Daddy."

"Wait a minute. I have some rules."

She sank back in her chair. "What else is new?"

He ignored the sarcasm. "First, you're not pulling a horse trailer all over the country. Second, you're not going alone. An adult has to go with you. I'll make the first two rodeos and we'll see if this horse performs like you think she can. You may not even like it."

"I will, Dad. I know I will."

He held up a finger. "But I'm still adamant about college. I'm going to insist that you go one year to see what life is like away from home with kids your own age. Deal?"

She thought about it for a minute. "But if I'm doing really good barrel racing why would I want to go to college?"

He cocked an eyebrow and he was sure he had a frowny face.

"All right." She slid out of her chair. "I know I'm not going to win this one, but you'll see. I'm going to be the best barrel racer ever."

His brother Jude, and Jude's son, Zane, came into the room and loaded their plates.

"Zane, if you're coming with me to school you better hurry," Eden said.

Zane stuffed scrambled eggs and bacon onto a biscuit. His grandma handed him a glass of orange juice and he downed it quickly, then followed his cousin to the door.

"I'm in a foul mood so you have to ride in the back-seat," Eden told Zane.

"Eden…"

"Okay, he can ride in the front seat, but he has to be quiet."

"Eden…"

"Okay. Okay. He can talk, but only ten words."

"Eden, this is a good way to put a stop to all talk of barrel racing. There's no need to be rude to Zane."

Zane winked at him. "Don't worry, Uncle Falcon. I have so much dirt on her I can make her sweat like a pig."

"Really?"

"Yeah. You know…" Eden grabbed him by his backpack and pulled him out the door.

"Isn't it great they get along so well?" Jude took a seat across from him.

"They get along fine," their mother said. "They're both good kids. Eden's trying to spread her wings and Zane is a sweet teddy bear."

"Said like a doting grandmother," Falcon replied, getting to his feet.

"What's the schedule today?" Jude asked. "We still have that load of young bulls to go to Dripping Springs and, of course, fences to mend."

Falcon took his plate to the sink. "You and Jericho can take the bulls and the rest of us can fix the fence on the McCray side. We don't want one animal to get through. It's too risky. We work on that fence all the time, but the McCrays always find a way to break it."

"They only do that to get back at us since the incident with Egan, but I do not want one of you to interact with them unless they go too far, and you know what I mean by that." Their mother made her views clear and they knew what she meant—to use their own judgment when dealing with the McCrays. But she never wanted her sons to back down and they knew that, too.

Falcon glanced out the window to see his daughter backing out of her parking spot. She was avidly talking to Zane, who had earphones on, blocking her out. They really were good friends, but with Eden's attitude it was hard to see that sometimes. She was very protective of her cousin, though. His daughter was a typical emotional teenager and her moods changed constantly. There was no way he'd ever be able to forget Leah. He saw her every day in their daughter.

A time to remember...

LEAH REBEL HAD SPENT years trying to deal with what she'd done, but each year a layer of guilt was added to her soul. There was no way to justify her actions, so she lived with an enormous burden of heartache and pain. At times she tried to explain to herself what had happened and she always fell short of making it convincing. If she couldn't make herself believe she wasn't a terrible person, how could she make Falcon believe?

It didn't matter, she told herself. The past was over and she couldn't go back and change it no matter how many times she wished she could. She had to go forward and that brought her to right now. To have a future she had to face her past. Which meant she had to face Falcon.

She pulled over to the side of the road to calm her nerves. Up ahead was the entrance to Rebel Ranch. It looked the same as it had the day she'd left, except the brown boards that flanked the entrance looked as if they'd just been painted. One summer she and Falcon had painted the boards. It had been fun, just the two of them making extra money during the summer.

They'd fallen in love in high school. The moment she'd set eyes on Falcon she knew she'd never love anyone else. She was young and naive and believed in true love. How stupid could she have been? Love was more than sex and attraction. It took a lot of give-and-take. Leah hadn't been ready to be tossed into the Rebel family. They'd treated her well, but she was used to a quiet life with her dad and her aunt.

After she'd discovered she was pregnant, Falcon had insisted they get married and they'd moved into his bedroom on the ranch. They'd had no privacy and life became difficult. The only time she had alone with him was in their bedroom. That special time had not given her the security she'd needed, especially with her hormones all over the place.

She wiped her sweaty palms down her black pants. Remembering was like scratching an itch. It only made it worse. And the more she remembered the more she hurt. Over and over the memories flooded her until she felt weak and wanted to turn the car around and drive back to Houston. But it had taken her seventeen-plus years to get to this point and she wasn't backing out now. No matter what awaited her on the other side of those board fences, she was ready to face it.

Just as she decided to drive forward she saw a red pickup headed for the entrance, dust billowing behind it. She was trapped, and waited for someone to recognize her. The truck rolled over the cattle guard and then stopped. The girl inside was talking to someone in the passenger seat.

Leah held her breath. It was her daughter: *Eden*. No

one needed to tell her that. She just knew. Her heart raced as she tried to see every detail of her face.

The two seemed to be arguing and then her daughter drove on, not once glancing her way. Leah was grateful for the distractions of a teenager. She backed up and then followed the red pickup. This might be her only chance to see her daughter. Not that she would introduce herself—she wouldn't be able to handle all that emotion. Just looking at her would be enough—for now.

The truck turned off Rebel Road and headed toward Horseshoe. Leah followed the truck all the way to the school. It had been a long time since she'd been there, but it still looked the same. The school was in the shape of a horseshoe with red brick halfway up the front of the metal buildings. Grades one through twelve went here when she was younger and she assumed they still did.

More memories surfaced. Falcon and her running to his truck to sneak away for an hour or so. Sitting in the stands, watching him play football and basketball. Wherever he was, she wanted to be. On the weekends, their favorite place was the ranch. They had a special spot on Yaupon Creek hidden back in the woods where they spent many hours making love. A pain shot through her. Why hadn't their love been enough?

Eden pulled into a parking spot and Leah parked some distance away, just far enough not to be noticed but close enough to see. Looking at her daughter was like looking into a mirror. Her daughter favored Leah, with long dark hair and a slim build. But Leah fervently hoped her daughter had more of a backbone than she ever had.

Eden was talking to the boy and Leah wondered who he was. One of Falcon's brothers must've gotten married and had a son, because he had the dark hair and features of a Rebel. He was maybe ten or eleven. So much had happened since Leah had been gone and she knew she would now be like a stranger to everyone.

Her daughter pulled off her three-quarter-length shirt, revealing a skimpy sleeveless top. The boy pointed a finger at her and Eden said something that evidently was not pleasant, because the boy made a face at her and then ran into the building.

Leah watched as Eden met a boy and they walked into the school together. It was like watching herself. She had done the same thing many times as a teenager. Her aunt believed in modesty and refused to let Leah wear skimpy clothes. The moment Leah made it to school she would remove the long-sleeved blouses.

Kate Rebel must be very strict with Eden. As much as it pained Leah to think it, she knew Kate had raised Leah's daughter. She couldn't see Falcon doing it. He was strong, masculine and had a traditional man's attitude that a woman's place was in the home.

Kate had finally gotten the daughter she'd always wanted, except Eden wasn't Kate's. Eden was Leah's. But Leah hadn't been a mother, a real mother, and it was the hardest thing she would ever have to admit. She'd changed, though, and she didn't know if anyone would believe her, especially Falcon. It didn't matter whether he did or not. She hadn't come for forgiveness. She'd come because she could no longer stay away.

She took a deep breath and picked up her phone to call the man she'd once loved with all her heart. She prayed that he would remember some of those times when they had been inseparable. If he'd let himself remember for a moment, maybe he would listen to what she had to say.

But knowing Falcon, he would want her to burn in hell.

Chapter Two

A time to meet...

Falcon glanced at the wagon-wheel clock on the wall. He and his mother handled the books for the ranch, and it took a lot of time. More time than he wanted to spend in an office. He'd rather be enjoying the outdoors.

Five years ago they'd built a new barn and made an updated office upstairs. He could see out over Rebel Ranch, but it wasn't the same as being out there.

His mother got up from her desk. "I'm going to check on the boys. It makes me nervous when they work so close to the McCray property."

Falcon leaned back in his leather chair. "I'll catch up with you as soon as Hancock calls. He wants to schedule a day to pick out the Hereford heifers for his ranch. It shouldn't take long."

As soon as his mother closed the door, Hancock called and set a date with Falcon. He hung up and the phone immediately rang again. Falcon answered without glancing at the caller ID. "Hello."

There was silence on the other end. "Hello, is anyone there?"

"Uh...uh... I..."

The voice was female so Falcon thought it was some-one looking for Paxton or Elias, which was a regular oc-currence. "You've reached Rebel Ranch. Who do you want to talk to?"

"Falcon, this is… Leah."

A line from an Alan Jackson song ran through his mind: *"Where were you when the world stopped turn-ing?"* For Falcon, everything stopped at that moment. He didn't care about a buyer wanting heifers or his brothers facing the McCrays. All he could hear was *This is Leah.*

He'd waited years for this call and now that it had come he was speechless. His nerves tightened like stretched barbed wire and his emotions were hard to contain. Anger, confusion and curiosity held him in a grip. He sucked air into his aching lungs.

"Falcon, are you still there?"

Her voice was just the same, soft with a Southern lilt. She'd been reared in Alabama and she never lost that cadence in her voice. It was sexy as hell, but today it only annoyed him.

"What do you want?"

"I'd like to talk."

"Where are you?"

"I'm at the new park in Horseshoe."

His heart pounded off his ribs in fear. Talking to Leah was the last thing he wanted to do, but she wasn't far from Eden and he had to make sure she didn't get any closer. "I'll be there in fifteen minutes."

Hanging up, he took a minute to absorb what had just happened. She was back. *Leah was back.* It happened so fast he was reeling. There could be only one thing she wanted and that was to see her daughter. And he was going to make sure that never happened. He would not let Leah hurt Eden like she had hurt him. That was his one thought as he ran for his truck.

LEAH PACED AROUND the park. She couldn't sit still. Her nerves felt as if they were tied into a big wad, like Christmas lights that could never be untangled. She looked around the park to calm herself. It sported colorful swings, slides, park benches and picnic areas. There was even a water playground for the kids. Water spewed up from several flat concrete fountains you could run through. She'd seen this in Houston and she never imagined they would have one in little Horseshoe, Texas.

Things had certainly changed since she'd been gone. She'd noticed a lot of new storefronts and several old stores had closed. Horseshoe would always be home, though. When she was twelve, her mother had died and she and her dad had moved there to live with his sister. Her dad had thought it would be good for Leah to have a woman around. In ways it had been, but in others it had been debilitating. *Why was she thinking about...?* A truck pulled up to the curb and her thoughts came to an abrupt stop. It was Falcon.

There was no mistaking him—tall, with broad shoulders and an intimidating glare. She swallowed hard as his long strides brought him closer. In jeans, boots and a Stetson he reminded her of the first time she'd met him in high school. Being new to the school system, she'd been shy and hadn't known a lot of the kids. It took her two years before she'd actually made friends and felt like part of a group. Falcon Rebel had been way out of that group. The girls swooned over him and the boys wanted to be like him: tough and confident.

One day she was sitting on a bench waiting for her

aunt to pick her up. Falcon strolled from the gym just
as he was now, with broad sure strides. She never knew
what made her get up from the bench, but as she did
she'd dropped her books and purse and items went everywhere. He'd stopped to help her and her hands shook
from the intensity of his dark eyes. From that moment
on there was no one for her but Falcon.

Now he stood about twelve feet from her and once
again she felt like that shy young girl trying to make
conversation. But this was so much more intense.

Be calm. Be calm. Be calm.

"I'm… I'm glad you came," she said, trying to main-
tain her composure because she knew the next few minutes were going to be the roughest of her life.

His eyes narrowed. "What do you want?" His words
were like hard rocks hitting her skin, each one intended
to import a message. His eyes were dark and angry, and
she wondered if she'd made the right decision in coming.

Gathering every ounce of courage she'd managed
to build over the years, she replied, "I want to see my
daughter."

He took a step closer to her. "Does the phrase 'over
my dead body' mean anything to you?"

At his uncompromising tone her courage faltered,
but she stood her ground. "I've already seen her, Falcon. But I would like the opportunity to visit with her
for a few minutes to explain about the past. She has a
right to know the truth."

"Where did you see her? And when?"

She slid her shaky hands into the pockets of her pants.
"I was coming to the ranch this morning and then I saw
a red pickup with a young woman. I knew it was her, so
I followed her to school."

"You didn't…"

"No, I didn't introduce myself. I wouldn't do that."

"Really? Like you would never walk out on her?"

She looked him in the eye. "I'd like to talk about that."

"There's nothing to talk about, Leah. It's done. It's in the past and it's best if you admit that and go back to wherever you came from."

"It's not done—"

"It is, and if you get anywhere near her, I will make your life a living hell."

Her heartbeat stumbled, but she remained steadfast. "You're not scaring me, Falcon. I'm her mother and I have a right to meet her and she has a right to know that I've thought about her every day since the day she was born."

He threw back his head and laughed a sound that chilled her to the bone. "That's a good one. If you think our daughter will believe that for a minute, you're dreaming. My daughter is much smarter than that."

"I know she hates me and I'm willing to risk her ire."

"Then you have no idea about your daughter's personality. She has a backbone, which is more than you ever had, and if you think 'I'm sorry' is going to work with her, then you're sipping something stronger than water."

Leah's heart skittered in panic. "I knew your mother would take care of her…"

"I took care of her." He jabbed a finger into his chest. "She was my daughter and I raised her, not my mother."

"What?"

"The crib stayed in my room and I got up with her during the night. I changed her diapers. I fed her and took her with me when I went out on the ranch."

"Why would you do that when your mother was there?"

"Because she wasn't my mother's responsibility. She was mine and yours. Since you bailed, there was only me and I wanted to make sure she knew she had one parent who loved her and would always be there for her."

A moan left her throat and she was unable to stop it. Falcon was never going to understand, and she didn't know if she had the strength to keep trying to explain.

"Her doctor sent us to a specialist in Austin to find out why she cried so much and after many tests, they found out she had something as simple as acid reflux. With medication, she did much better and was soon able to sleep during the night. But it was rough for a while. The only way she could sleep was on my chest. I was so afraid I was going to roll over and crush her, so I slept lightly and didn't get much rest. But we got through it. It's a shame her mother wasn't there when she took her first step holding on to my finger or when she started running instead of walking, chasing me out the door. She never wanted me out of her sight. I wonder why that was, Leah? Could it be she knew at that early age her mother had abandoned her?"

"Don't say that."

He stared at her and she felt as if he was looking right into her soul. If he was, he could see all the scars, all the pain and all the sorrow. But there was no sympathy on his face. She didn't believe for one minute that this meeting would be easy and she wouldn't let his words discourage her from seeing her daughter.

"Does the truth hurt?"

Her eyes met his. "Yes, it does. Is that what you wanted to hear? I've been hurting for a long time."

He shrugged. "Doesn't matter to me. I want you out of Horseshoe just as soon as possible." He swung toward his truck.

"I want a divorce."

He swung back, his eyes dark and disturbing. She took a step backward.

"That's the real reason you came back, isn't it? You've found someone and want to remarry."

"It's just time to end our marriage."

He took several steps toward her and she had to force herself not to take another step away from him. "Here's another saying, Leah, 'when hell freezes over.' That's when I'll give you a divorce to marry someone else. You have put me through hell and I'm not going to make life easier for you now. So go back to wherever you found what you were searching for. God only knows what that was. I gave you my heart and it wasn't enough. So if you're looking for forgiveness, you're asking the wrong man. I'll never forgive you for what you did to us."

She swallowed the sob in her throat. "Could we talk about that time?"

"The time for talk is over. I really don't want to hear your excuses. Nothing can excuse what you did to a three-month-old little girl who needed her mother."

"Falcon…"

"You know how many nights I lay awake with Eden on my chest, waiting for the phone to ring, waiting to hear from her mother, waiting for her to let us know she was okay? The call never came until today, when her mother wants something. How selfish is that? Have a good life, Leah. You will never be free of me." He strolled off to his truck, his back rigid, his stride rapid and determined to carry him as far away from her as possible.

Leah sank onto the bench because her shaky legs would no longer hold her. She tried to breathe, tried to think and desperately tried not to pass out. She focused on the water spewing up from the pavement. Splat. Splat. Splat. Calming. Soothing. The dizziness eased and she sucked in a deep breath, praying she would never show this weakness in front of Falcon. He said it was over. It wasn't. She wasn't leaving Horseshoe until she saw her daughter. Falcon may intimidate her, but he would not break her.

Her rights as a mother had been severed with her callous actions, but her rights as a woman—someone who had learned and grown and fought for a life—would never be severed. Not until she drew her last breath.

FALCON WAS SO angry his breaths came in gulps. He pressed his foot down on the accelerator and broke the speed limit all the way to the ranch. At the barn, he slammed on the brakes and the King Ranch Ford spun and stopped about three feet from the barn. Dust blanketed the truck. He jumped out and went into the barn to get his horse.

Opening the corral, he whistled for Titan, his black gelding. The horse galloped toward him, eager to ride. Within minutes he'd saddled up and he headed out to join his brothers. He kneed Titan and the horse responded with a speed that always elated Falcon. He rode through the valley and over gently rolling hills as if his life depended on it. In a way it did.

Realizing he was pushing Titan too hard, he pulled up and slid from the saddle. Sinking down by a large oak, he took a moment to collect his chaotic thoughts. How dare she! How dare she come back and demand to see Eden? She had no right and he would never allow her anywhere near their daughter.

He ran his hands down his face and took a long breath, trying not to even think how damn gorgeous she still looked. She could've at least put on weight, showed aging on her face or sported a few gray hairs, but she was as beautiful as she'd ever been. And she'd met someone else. That gnawed at his insides. How dare she!

Getting to his feet, he resolved not to let her ruin one more day of his life. He'd spent too many hours thinking about her, but not anymore. He swung into the saddle and rode toward the northeast pasture. From a distance he could see something was wrong. Gunnar and Malachi McCray were on their side of the fence and his brothers on theirs. A heated conversation was evident as Elias waved his arms. Grandpa watched from his horse. His mother wasn't there, and he wondered why.

Falcon dismounted before Titan came to a complete stop. "What's going on?"

Elias swung toward him. "They've been standing there gawking at us all morning and I'm getting tired of it." Elias held up his fists at Gunnar. "You want a piece of me, just come across that fence."

"Stop it," Falcon said to Elias and moved closer to Gunnar. "Is there a problem?"

"Just want to make sure you don't cross the line, Rebel."

Elias pointed a finger at him. "It's you who's always crossing our fence lines and cutting them and killing our calves. You're not brave enough to cross it now, are you?"

"Neither are you," Gunnar shot back.

It was all the incentive Elias needed as he made to jump over the fence, but Quincy and Egan caught him and pulled him back.

"Let me go. Let me go! I'll kick his ass."

"Stop it," Falcon said once again and Elias quit fighting his brothers.

Grandpa kneed his horse a little closer to the fence. "You know, boy, if brains were dynamite, you wouldn't have enough to blow your ears off."

"Grandpa." Falcon didn't need his grandfather getting in on the fight, but then his grandpa always loved one.

"Just look around you," Grandpa said. "We've got you outnumbered. What kind of fool would take on this many Rebels?"

Falcon focused his attention on Gunnar. "We spend more time on this fence than any other on our property because the McCrays are breaking it on purpose. If it's cut one more time, I'm stringing a hot wire through here. Try cutting that."

"Hot damn, now we're talking." Elias threw back his head and laughed.

Their mother rode up with a picnic basket strapped onto her horse. Evidently, she'd brought lunch. She took the situation in at a glance and asked, "Is there a problem?"

"Yes, Miz Rebel," Gunnar replied. "You need to teach your boys some manners."

"My boys have good manners, but I'm not sure about the McCrays, who cause mischief for no reason."

"Oh, we got reason."

The situation was getting out of control and Falcon

wouldn't have his mother caught in the middle. She'd been through too much.

"Get on your horses and leave," he said, pointing at the McCrays. "That's the last warning."

"This isn't the end of it, Rebel!" Gunnar shouted as he mounted his horse. Malachi followed suit.

"It never is."

The McCrays rode away and Falcon spoke to his brothers. "Let's get back to work."

"What caused this?" His mother wanted to know.

They all looked at Elias.

"They've been staring at us all morning and I got tired of it."

"Son, it takes a strong man to walk away from a fight."

"Well, I'm not one of them."

"Sadly, that's true."

"Ah, Mom."

"Try to use a little discretion, please."

"Yes, ma'am." Elias hung his head.

"Now, let's have lunch," his mother said, and they all gathered under a big oak. For September, the heat of summer still lingered and they were glad for the breeze that cooled their sweaty skin.

Grandpa leaned against the oak, his hat on the grass. "Did I ever tell you boys about the time I took on six men and lived to tell about it?"

"Abe, please, let the boys rest before they go back to work."

"You're one bossy—"

Falcon cleared his throat and Grandpa's attention was diverted. His mother and grandfather had never gotten along and after his father's death their relationship had taken a turn for the worse. He spent half his time try-ing to cool their tempers. Grandpa was long-winded and loved to talk and his mother hated it. He wondered what it was like to be part of a normal family. His thoughts swayed to Leah and he immediately pushed them away. He couldn't think about her now.

With lunch over, his mother packed up and headed back to the ranch with Grandpa. Of course, they wouldn't speak. Once they reached the ranch, Grandpa would go to his house and his mother would go to hers. Yep, that was the Rebel family.

"I'm working with Quincy," Elias said. "Egan hums now and it annoys the crap out of me. Happyitis has gotten to him."

Egan caught Elias around the neck. "I'll sing to you, then."

"Falcon!" Elias called as Egan dragged him toward the Polaris Ranger loaded with supplies.

It was good to see Egan happy. He'd found happiness with Rachel and they had gotten married in July. After he had been wrongly sent to prison they'd worried he would never find his way back to any type of life. All it took was a woman who loved him to bring him out of the darkness.

Quincy picked up his hat from the ground. "A couple more hours and this fence should be fixed for good."

Falcon stared at his brother. They were fourteen months apart and similar in size and looks, except Quincy had his mother's softer personality. Falcon had inherited the roughness of his father.

"Stop putting ideas into my daughter's head."

Quincy frowned. "What?"

"You know I want her to go to college. What's all this about her barrel racing?"

"Do you ever listen to Eden? She loves this ranch and she doesn't want to leave. Any idea of rodeoing was strictly hers."

Falcon glanced off to the hot noon sun. "I know. I just want her to be a normal teenager instead of always hanging around this ranch with her uncles. I want her to be a girl."

"Well, then, you shouldn't have raised her as a boy." Quincy slapped him on the back. "But don't worry, those girl genes are there. Give her time."

"I want her to experience life away from here, but it scares me to death that I'm going to lose her. I know that sounds crazy."

"You sound like a father. Just listen to your daughter. That's all you have to do." Quincy walked off to join Egan and Elias.

Everyone always called him strong, but Falcon didn't know if he was strong enough to deal with the Leah situation. The underlying fear he was going to lose his daughter to her mother was something he couldn't shake.

Chapter Three

A time for little girls...

Falcon tossed and turned, unable to sleep. Every time he closed his eyes he saw Leah's face and he knew she wasn't going to give up on seeing their daughter. She could easily go to the school and meet her afterward. All his threats didn't mean a thing. He stood to lose everything he loved.

His thoughts tortured him and he got up. Slipping on his robe, a melancholy smile touched his lips. No one, except his mother, wore a robe before Eden was born. With a little girl in the house, they couldn't walk around in their underwear. A lot of things had changed with the birth of Eden. She'd been the light in John Rebel's eyes. He would hold her at night while watching television until she fell asleep and then Falcon would put her in her crib.

After his father's death, Eden would wander around the house calling, "Papa!" She was only four but she missed her grandfather. At the memory, Falcon's chest ached. He missed his dad more than he could ever explain to anyone. He blamed himself for not doing more to help his dad to stop drinking. But after killing Ezra McCray, John Rebel had demons that only he could face.

Falcon headed downstairs to get Leah's number off the landline. Everyone used their cell phones these days and there was only a landline in the den, the kitchen and the office. He didn't turn on a light because he didn't want to disturb anyone. The kids had school tomorrow and they'd been in bed for over an hour. The moonlight shone through the windows as he made his way down the stairs.

In the den, he searched the caller ID and found the number. He could see fine by his cell phone as he added Leah to his contacts. To get what he wanted he'd have to give a little, but his top priority was protecting Eden, and that included from her mother.

It was after eleven and he hesitated to call her now. It could wait until morning. He heard a noise and a click. Someone was coming through the back door very quietly. He tensed. Everyone was in bed. Who was it?

He waited and saw a figure tiptoe across the den to the staircase. No mistaking the person. It was his daughter. She'd snuck out. How often did she do that? He trusted her and that trust was severely shaken.

He clicked on the desk lamp.

Eden swung around, her eyes huge in her startled face. Her hair was tousled and her blouse was opened slightly, revealing her breasts. Anger surged through him but he managed to control it.

"Oh... Dad. You scared me."

"I bet. Where have you been?"

"Um... I...um..."

"Come on, think of a good lie, something you can get past your ol' dad." He got up and walked through the house to the dining room. Peeping through the blinds, he could see taillights come on as a vehicle neared the cattle guard.

"Who's that leaving?"

She made a face. "Okay, you caught me."

Falcon walked back to the desk and sat down. "Who did you sneak out to see when I thought you were safely in bed?"

"Well, now, don't freak out." She moved closer to the desk.

"I don't freak out."

"Yeah, I know. And that's really weird, Dad. Everyone freaks out every now and then."

He couldn't, not when he had the family and Rebel Ranch on his shoulders. He had to be level-headed and rational at all times.

"I'm almost at the edge so you better start talking."

She ran her fingers over some papers on the desk. "Well, Dad, it was Brandon."

"The boy with the tattoos, the earring and the motorcycle?"

"Yeah."

Falcon bit his tongue because if he ever needed a clear head, he needed it now. "Why did he come this late at night?"

"Just listen, please."

"I'll try."

"I like him and we talk a lot in school. Today he asked me to go out on Saturday and I said I couldn't because I was going to be practicing with Dancer. Then I had a class with Kyle Weatherford and he said he had tickets to see Luke Bryan in Austin and wanted to know if I'd like to go with him. I said I would love to see Luke

Bryan, and Brandon heard me and got his feelings hurt. But he didn't hear the rest of what I said to Kyle. It was the same thing I told Brandon—I couldn't go because I had other plans. I couldn't find Brandon to explain."

She sighed. "This is a long story. Are you sure you want to hear all of it?"

"Every word."

"Brandon texted me about ten and wanted to know the real reason I wouldn't go out with him and I explained what happened. He said he wanted to talk to me and I said we could do that tomorrow. Then he said he was at the cattle guard and wanted to talk now. So I put on my clothes and met him outside. It's as simple as that."

Falcon leaned forward, proud of himself for remaining calm. "From the looks of your hair and your blouse, I'd say things got a little heated."

"Oh, Dad." She came around the desk and sat on the edge and he noted she had on her bunny slippers. "I don't want to talk about this with you. It's boy stuff."

"You'll soon be eighteen years old, a woman, and I realize that. I just have one question. Are you having sex with Brandon?"

She hung her head. Her hair covered her face and he couldn't see what she was thinking. "No. He wants to, but I'm nervous."

At her pitiful voice, all this anger left him. Now he had to be a father, and this part of parenting scared the crap out of him. "Why?"

She flipped back her hair. "I don't want to be like my mother and get pregnant in high school. I want to make better choices and I want to be in love."

Damn. He must've done something right. She was

saying everything he wanted to hear. "Your mother and I were in love. I want you to know that."

"Then why did she leave?"

"I can't speak for your mother, but the pregnancy was rough on her and she had problems afterward. Problems I should have been more aware of. I regret that now."

"If she loved us, she would've come back."

"Oh, baby." He pulled her onto his lap as if she was three years old. "She did love us."

"No, she didn't." Eden snuggled closer into him. "Do you ever wonder if she's alive?"

"Yeah." *She is. How do I tell you that?* He thought it best to change the subject for now.

"So, do you love this Brandon?"

"I don't know. Sometimes I like it when he touches me and other times it makes me feel uncomfortable."

"If it makes you uncomfortable—"

"It's just… I like kissing him and all, but when it gets really heavy, I get nervous and scared and that's when Brandon gets mad."

"Don't ever let a boy pressure you into sex."

"Did you pressure my mother?"

It was on the tip of his tongue to lie, but since his daughter was being so honest he had to do the same. "Yes."

"Why do boys do that?"

"It's hard to explain, baby, especially to my own daughter. Why don't I make an appointment with the pediatrician and you can ask her these difficult questions. I'm sure she would be happy to go over this with you."

"The pediatrician? Dad, seriously? I'm seventeen years old and I know about the birds and the bees. Re-member we talked about it when I got my period and you took me to see the pediatrician then so she could explain intimate stuff that made you sweat?"

He remembered it vividly and he had been sweating bullets.

"I know about sex. My friends and I talk about it all the time. Kelley and Michelle are on birth control, but I'm not ready for that. Sex…well, it just makes me nervous." ·

"You can talk to Rachel or Lacey. They're in the family now."

"I don't need to talk to anyone. It's about me and the way I feel."

"Grandma is always here if you need her."

"Dad, Grandma would really freak out."

Falcon smiled. "Grandma's a little old-fashioned, but I'm sure she would answer any questions you have."

"Forget I said anything," she mumbled.

"When it comes to boys, I want you to be very sure of what you want. I know most girls your age are sexually active, but you have to understand, as your dad, I'd rather you waited until you've found someone special."

"I'll probably die a virgin."

He squeezed her. "I doubt that."

She rested her head in the crook of his shoulder. "Daddy, I don't want to go away to college. I want to stay here with you, Grandma, Grandpa, the uncs and Zane."

At that little-girl's voice, Falcon knew he'd failed as a parent. He'd protected and sheltered Eden, as his mother and brothers had. Now she was afraid to leave the nest.

"Is this what barrel racing is about?"

"I don't know. Maybe."

"Baby, just about every kid wants to go to college. It's

lots of fun, I'm told. Parties, staying up as late as you want, being an adult and making your own decisions."

"Kelley is going and so is Michelle. They can hardly wait."

Besides her conflicting thoughts about sex, something else was holding Eden back, keeping her from enjoying these years.

"What is it, baby? Why can't you enjoy this with your friends?"

"Because…because when I go, you'll be all alone."

"What are you talking about? My brothers, Mom, Grandpa and Zane are here and enough work to keep me busy for the rest of my life."

"But it's always been just you and me and when I graduate, I won't be here anymore in case you need me."

"Eden, baby, that's what life is about—changes. Nothing stays the same. I want you to grow up, be independent, but most of all I want you to be happy. And maybe every now and then you can come visit dear ol' dad."

Eden giggled and then became silent. "Do you remember that book you bought me when I was a kid about a genie granting wishes? I wanted to find a genie in a bottle so she could grant me my wish, and my wish was that my mother would come home."

A lump clogged Falcon's throat. He should tell her about Leah. Eden needed her mother now more than ever. But he had to be sure of Leah's motives.

"Wouldn't it be great if we could pick a time in our lives that we were happy and we could live in that moment forever? Do you know what time I'd pick?" She twisted her head to look at him.

"I have no idea."

"It would be when I was little and Papa was alive. I

know some people say I can't remember because I was too small, but I do. I can remember the sound of his boots on the tiled floor when he came home and him shouting, 'Eden. Where's my Eden?' I can remember the excitement in my chest when I heard his big voice. I'd shout, 'I'm here, Papa,' and run to meet him. He'd grab me and throw me in the air and hold me up until I could almost touch the ceiling. Then he'd sit me on his shoulder and I felt on top of the world. I was happy and Grandma smiled a lot then and all the uncs were in good moods. But then he died and everything changed. No one seemed to be happy anymore. I don't like change."

She rested her head on his shoulder again and they didn't speak for a moment. It was uncanny how she remembered that. It happened just the way she'd said. His father had so many people who loved him. Why hadn't he fought to live instead of giving in to the liquor? Sometimes that angered Falcon. And saddened him, too.

His dad had been the strongest man Falcon had ever known. But he also had his weaknesses and Falcon became very aware of them after the shooting. His dad would work all day on the ranch and then after supper he would retire to his room with a bottle of Scotch. He would drink until he passed out. That was the only way he could sleep.

When Eden was born, his routine changed and Falcon had hoped for better things. John Rebel would spend time with his granddaughter, but as soon as she'd go to sleep, he'd go to his room with a bottle. One morning his mom had found him on their deck with an empty bottle in his lap. He had died sometime during the night. It was a shock to everyone. John's sons had thought he was invincible and could beat anything. But they'd been wrong. Admitting that had taken more courage than any of them thought they'd had. Life after their father hadn't been easy.

"What time would you choose to live in, Daddy?"

"Eden, that's silly."

"No, it isn't. I told you mine and now you have to tell me yours."

He didn't have to think about it. "I'd choose that time when your mom and I were teenagers and it was just the two of us. The world ceased to exist. We lived just for each other."

"See, that's what makes me nervous. You and my mom were so in love, but it wasn't real. It only lasted for a little while. How do you know if it's real? I don't want to get hurt like that—like she hurt you."

"Oh, baby girl." He hugged her. "There are no guarantees in this world. You just have to go with your heart. I don't regret one moment I spent with your mom. She gave me you."

"Ah, Daddy, you're gonna make me cry."

"One day you're going to meet a guy, and you're going to feel a special connection like you've never felt before. I can't explain exactly what it is, but you'll know when it happens. He'll be all you ever think about and when he touches you, you won't be uncomfortable. It'll be natural and everything will fall into place. Love is something you have to work on. Both parties have to work on it, not just one. A lot of things can go wrong. If the relationship falls apart, it's the way it was meant to be. You can't beat yourself up. You have to live in the moment. Remember that genie thing and all. Very few people get it right, Eden, but we all play the game because it's worth it."

She kissed his cheek. "I have the best dad in the world. Sometimes he's grouchy but I still love him."

"Love you, too, baby girl. Now you better go to bed. You have school tomorrow."

She got up from his lap and stood there in tight jeans and bunny slippers. A woman, but the little girl was hanging on with all her might. Falcon would miss that little girl. But he was looking forward to getting to know the woman. She had values and principles and he hoped he had something to do with that. He knew in his heart that whatever she had to face down the road, she had the strength to do it. Even meeting her mother for the first time.

"You know what, Dad?" she said walking toward the stairs. "I'm going to barrel race, go to college and have sex."

"There's no rush on the last part. Take your time and make your dad happy."

She laughed and ran up the stairs. Falcon stood with a weary sigh and clicked off the lamp. He had a big decision to make, but he knew he'd already made it. Eden deserved to know her mother. Or at least to meet her. He wouldn't keep that from her.

Falcon headed toward his mother's room. She hadn't gotten up with the noise or the light and that bothered him. Her door was slightly ajar and he peeped in. She was curled up in the bed. Evidently, she'd heard them and gone back to bed, not wanting to interrupt.

On the way to his room, the responsibilities of life hit him. He had to make right decisions for everyone, but most of all for Eden.

In his room, he sat on the bed and took his cell out of the pocket of his robe. It was after twelve and Leah was probably asleep. He'd call tomorrow. But something in him couldn't wait.

It was answered almost immediately. "Falcon."

"Yes. We need to talk."

"When?"

"Tomorrow."

"Have you told Eden?"

"No, I want to be sure of your motives and I want answers. I want to know where you've been all these years and why you couldn't pick up the phone to call your family. I want every damn detail, Leah. You're not seeing your daughter until you give me those answers."

"I'm not asking anything of you. I just want to see my daughter for a few minutes. You don't have to grill me for that."

"A few minutes? That's all your daughter means to you? A few minutes?"

"Don't make this difficult."

He gritted his teeth. "You have a whole new life planned and your daughter doesn't fit in. Is that it?"

"It's too late, Falcon. Can't you see that?"

"No. All I see is a selfish woman thinking only of herself."

There was complete silence on the other end.

"Leah?"

"I don't know what you want me to say. Eden is seventeen years old and I can't just suddenly become a mother. I'm sure she doesn't want that and I'm sure she hates me by now. Just let me have a few minutes and I'll disappear out of your lives."

"Oh, it's easy for you to disappear. Why don't you try staying for a while and facing your responsibilities?"

"When can I see her?" she asked instead of answering.

"Not until we talk. Where are you staying?"

"At a hotel in Temple." She gave him the name and room number.

"I'll be there at ten in the morning," he said, and clicked off. She wanted to bend him to her will, but that wasn't happening. He'd allow the few minutes she so desperately needed with her daughter. Not for Leah, though. For his daughter. Eden deserved at least that much. But he would never give Leah a divorce to marry someone else. That would be his ultimate revenge.

Chapter Four

A time for truth...

Falcon woke up at 5 a.m. and the morning seemed to drag. He had to call Eden three times before she got up. The late night had caught up with her. After all the craziness of the morning, one thought kept him focused: it was time to talk to Leah.

Rebel Ranch was getting ready for the fall roundup and he really needed to be home. His brothers gave him a funny look when he said he would catch them later. Of course, they had questions. Falcon was always on top of everything that happened at the ranch, but today he wasn't in the mood to tell them about Leah. That would come later. His mother must've sensed his mood, because she didn't ask questions. He was grateful for that.

At nine o'clock he was finally on his way to Temple. He called Leah to tell her he would be there early. She said she would order coffee and he started to tell her not to bother. But he might need something strong to get him through the morning.

The hotel was one of the nicer ones in Temple. He walked to the elevator and went up to the third floor. It didn't take him long to find her room. He knocked and it opened almost immediately.

He paused at the sight of her in a slim-fitting black dress and a red belt circling her tiny waist. Her dark hair hung to her shoulders in a tousled style. On her feet were strappy high heels. This wasn't the Leah he knew in jeans and sneakers. This woman was a stranger to him.

She held the door wider. "Come in."

He followed her into what was obviously a suite with two rooms—a living area and a bedroom.

"Have a seat." She motioned to the sofa.

The room was stylish with ornate furniture, and he'd guess it had cost a bundle to book. How could she afford this? Obviously her life had been good and for the first time, he realized that the young girl he had married had long been gone in more ways than one.

He sat down and placed his hat beside him. She stood a few feet away, looking as beautiful as he'd ever seen her. If he didn't know her so well he would think she was as cool as a winter breeze, but he recognized the tension in her body and the nervousness in the way she kept glancing toward the door.

"Where have you been for over seventeen years?" He didn't see any reason to postpone the inevitable. A knock at the door stalled her answer.

A waiter brought in a carafe of coffee and a teapot. That puzzled him, but not for long. She poured a cup of tea for herself.

"You drink tea now?"

"Chamomile. It helps me to relax." She handed him a cup of coffee and then she stirred her tea.

He held the cup with both hands and forced himself to

calm down so he wouldn't break it into a million pieces. "Where have you been, Leah?"

Taking a seat in a wingback chair, she replied, "It's a long story."

"I've got time."

She took a sip of tea and placed the cup back on the tray. "I...I don't know where to start."

"How about the day you left."

"Okay." She took a deep breath. "I was up all night with Eden. I couldn't get her to stop crying and I was so frustrated and felt helpless as a mother. When you held her, or Kate, she would stop, so there had to be something wrong with me. I thought I was hurting her in some way."

"That's crazy."

She glared at him. "Are you going to make snide comments or are you going to listen?"

"I'll listen."

"I never told you about my mother. It was difficult for me to tell anyone."

"You said she died in an accident when you were twelve."

"Yes. A terrible accident. See, my mom was bipolar and she would go into these violent rages that were hard to deal with." Leah reached for her cup and took a swallow. "When she was in these rages, she always wanted to hurt someone, and I was always around so it was usually me. She broke my arm, my ribs, my collarbone and gave me more bruises than I can remember. I finally learned to hide from her and that was probably the only thing that saved my life. My dad just worked more and more. One day a guy cut her off on the highway and she followed him to a gas station ranting and raving. He pulled a handgun from the glove compartment and shot her. She died at the scene."

Falcon was stunned and his heart ached for that little girl who grew up so afraid. He never knew she suffered like that. It was probably the reason she was so shy and quiet.

"Why couldn't you tell me that?"

"I don't know." She placed the cup back on the tray. "I just wanted to forget it and start a new life in Horseshoe. You see, I didn't want to remember I had that kind of mother. But when Eden wouldn't stop crying I thought I was hurting my child like my mother had hurt me. That day when she cried and cried, I had this urge to put my hand over her mouth to stop the crying. As soon as the thought entered my head, I knew I had to get away. I just had to get out of the house for a couple of days to prove to myself that I wasn't a terrible person."

"Leah…"

"Eden finally went to sleep. I went downstairs and told your mother I was going out for a while and for her to listen for Eden. I got in my car and drove away."

"Where did you go?"

Leah looked down at her clasped hands in her lap. "I was going to my cousin's in Houston. I thought I could stay there until I got my head straight."

"I called Nancy and she said she hadn't heard from you, in case you're planning to lie. I called her for six solid months and every time she said the same thing— she didn't know where you were."

"I never made it to her house."

"What happened?" A sense of dread came over him. He had the same feeling the day he'd heard his dad screaming for their mother. Falcon had been feeding the horses when his dad had raced toward the barn with a bloody Jude and Phoenix in his arms. Whatever Leah had to say, he knew it was as bad as what had happened that day. Instinctively, he tensed as he prepared himself to listen to the rest of her story.

"I drove to Austin, to the bus station. I left my car about a block away. I'm not sure why I did that. It's not clear in my head why I didn't just drive to Nancy's. But I think I was afraid you would come after me and make me go back when I wasn't ready. I really needed some time."

"The police called the next week and I picked up the car. There was no trace of you and the police concluded that you just wanted to get out of an unhappy marriage."

"It wasn't like that."

"What was it like?"

"I loved you with all my heart, but I couldn't deal with the baby and the crying and the fear that I was going to hurt her. Living with your family didn't help, either. It was overwhelming."

He swallowed, knowing part of her problem was his fault. "What happened next?"

"I took the bus to Houston fully intending to go to Nancy's. The pay phone was broken at the bus station and the guy said there was one at the convenience store across the street. It was raining and I waited for it to let up before I ran down the street, but it started pouring again and I could hardly see. The light was yellow and cars were stopping so I darted across the intersection. One car didn't stop and it hit me. I woke up a year later."

"What?" The dread in his stomach became a burning ache and permeated his body. He felt as if he was on fire.

"Most of that time is a blur, but Miss Hattie…"

"Who's Hattie?"

"Hattience Thornwall, but everyone calls her Hattie. She's the lady who hit me. She was seventy-five years old and felt guilty over what had happened. Her car hit me and knocked me into the intersection, where another car ran over me. I had two broken legs, my chest was crushed and I had severe head injuries—the side of my face slid on the pavement, ripping away the skin and part of my ear, and one eye bulged out. Once in the ER they worked on my chest and my head, the most life-threatening injuries."

Falcon stood up, needing to move as his emotions swamped him. "Why didn't someone call me? I'm your next of kin."

"Someone stole my purse at the scene and no one knew who I was. I had no identity. I was Jane Doe number seventy-two."

"In this day and age there had to have been some way to identify you! What about your wedding ring? Our names were engraved on the inside."

"I was told they cut it off my swollen hand and it must have gotten thrown away by mistake. The authorities ran my picture in the paper, but no one came forward. The picture was after the accident and Miss Hattie said I probably didn't look like myself."

"You talk of this woman with fondness and she caused you all this misery."

"Yes, it's a little confusing, but it was part my fault, too. Please listen to the whole story."

He sat down again, unable to do anything else.

"They didn't expect me to live, and the hospital had to get a court order to take me off the ventilator. Miss Hattie fought this, but she lost. They removed it and were shocked when I could breathe on my own. Since they didn't know who I was and I had no insurance, they moved me to an indigent hospital. After many weeks, I was still unconscious, so they prepared to put me in a state institution. Once again Miss Hattie objected to this. She had me moved to a private facility and she paid the bills."

"That was generous."

"Yes, the nurses said she visited at least three times a week and always brought fresh flowers for my room. One year and two days later I opened my eyes and the first word I said was Eden. I had no idea who she was or where I was and I quickly drifted into a deep sleep again. I kept waking up, confused and disoriented. The nurses said I kept calling for Falcon and asked who he was. I had no idea, but I knew he was important to me."

A catch in his throat kept him from responding.

"Little by little my memory started to come back, but my muscles had atrophied and I couldn't even feed myself. I was totally helpless."

"If you knew your name, why didn't someone call me then?"

"My memory didn't come back all at once. Bits and pieces came to me and it was five years before I could put all those pieces together. In the meantime they had to concentrate on my legs because they didn't operate on them at the time of the accident. They were more concerned about my chest and my head and they didn't think I would make it anyway. Nor did they think I could live through the surgery. Anyway, I had several operations on my legs. It was a long road to recovery. Miss Hattie hired therapists and they worked diligently with me to teach me to use my muscles and legs again. And David repaired my face."

"David?" By the tone of her voice he knew this man was special to her.

"He's Miss Hattie's son and a plastic surgeon. It took numerous skin grafts but he did an amazing job. He even repaired my ear."

Falcon looked closely at her face and saw the beautiful woman she'd always been. There was no way to tell she'd been through such a horrific tragedy. There were so many questions in his head that he didn't even know where to start. The anger that he carried through the years wasn't there anymore. All he felt was empathy for what she'd been through.

"When did you realize you had a husband and a child in Horseshoe?"

She glanced down at her hands in her lap. "It was probably about six years before I had the full picture."

"And yet, you didn't call home or ask anyone else to. You let us believe the worst."

She kept staring down at her hands. "I know it's hard to understand. But I woke up a completely different person from the shy, timid Leah that you knew. I always had this feeling that no one loved me until you filled that empty place in me. But then I met Miss Hattie and David and they loved me unconditionally. After two and a half years in the facility, Miss Hattie took me home to her house and hired a nurse and a therapist for me. I was on a walker and I couldn't believe that she cared that much about me. We became the best of friends."

"You had a family in Horseshoe who loved you."

"I know," she murmured, still looking at her hands. "After my memory came back, a day didn't go by that I didn't think of you and Eden, but I had so many health problems and I didn't want to be a burden to you. I kept thinking once I got better I could go home. The surgeries to my face took a long time and it took forever for me to regain my strength. Each day was a struggle and I didn't want to put the responsibility on you and your family."

He stood up again as emotions hit him like a slap in the face. Why couldn't she come home? He didn't understand that. "When we got married, the vows said in sickness and in health. Did you forget that?"

She looked at him for the first time. "I caused all this misery to myself because I didn't have the courage to care for my child. I ran away instead. That's all on me and it was hard to live with. I didn't want to come home until I was fully well. But then things happened."

"Like what?"

"Miss Hattie had a stroke and I couldn't leave then. She'd been so good to me and I had to stay to help her. She took care of me and I had to take care of her. She was the loving mother I never had. And David and I grew closer. He was just as nice and loving as his mother. I never had that kind of love in my life."

It finally dawned on Falcon. "Oh, this David is who you want to marry. This David is why you want a divorce. This David is why you have finally come home, only to leave again. That's not fair to Eden and it's not fair to me."

"I know, that makes me a really bad person. I'm not asking for forgiveness. I'm not asking to be a part of your life again. I'm only asking for a few minutes with my daughter."

"What will that help, Leah? She's seventeen and dealing with all kinds of conflicting emotions. I can tell you she will not understand, so why put her through this?"

She stood, her eyes a wave of frosty green. "I'm prepared for that. I can't go forward with my life until I talk to her."

Looking at her expensive clothes and artfully made-up face, he had to ask, "Your life is good, I take it."

"Yes. I took some business courses and I work in David's office."

"How nice. Doesn't Miss Hattie need you?" He couldn't keep the sarcasm out of his voice because the anger was starting to come back like a tidal wave and he couldn't stop it. He had to wonder if she thought he had nerves of steel and he could take all this with a smiling face and have-a-good-life attitude. He was far from feeling that.

"Miss Hattie died a few months ago and she left me her house and many good memories."

His gut clenched. Didn't they have good memories? Was that what she was implying? He drew a heavy breath. Almost eighteen years and he remembered everything, even things that hurt. But it was clear that she didn't. The thought caused an unsettling emotion—green-eyed jealousy.

"I guess you share this house with David?"

"No. He has his own place. David and Miss Hattie saved my life and we became a family. They spent so many hours helping me to get well and to live a full life. I never knew anyone could be so loving and giving. I know you don't like to hear that, but it's the truth. I didn't mean for this to happen. It just did and we both have to move on now."

He wasn't going to go gently into this divorce. No

way. He wasn't built that way. "Do you think it was easy
for me, Leah, raising a baby? And then my father died
and I had to take over the running of the ranch while
taking care of a four-year-old. There weren't enough
hours in the day, but Eden was always my top priority."

She gasped. "John died?"

"Yes, four years after you left the ranch. It was hard
on all of us, but especially for Eden because she loved
her Papa."

"Falcon, I'm so sorry. I know how you felt about him."

What was he supposed to say? There were no words.
"I know you've been through a lot, but I'll never understand how you can regain your memory and still stay
away from your daughter. It doesn't matter how you felt
about me. Eden deserved more. I can tell you for a fact
if I was hurt and away from home, getting back to my
child would've been my main goal. I'll never understand
how you could have ignored her."

Leah held a hand to her forehead. "Please, I…"

He threw up a hand. "Okay. I can't change your mind.
I see you have some kind of plan that you have to see
Eden. I can't really stop you because Eden is almost
an adult and I'd rather be there to protect her. So you
can have a few minutes if it means that much to you to
start this new life." He ran a shaky hand through his
hair. "This is not easy for me even if you think I have
ice water in my veins. You're my wife and in my mind
you've always been my wife. All these years haven't
changed that. You owe me, Leah—for all the years you
weren't in our lives, for all the nights you weren't in
my bed and for all the misery you put me through. You
owe me, and if you want me to be happy for this new
love that you've found, then you don't know me at all."

She stared at him, tears glistening in her eyes. He steeled himself against them.

"I'm sorry. What do you want from me?"

The moment she asked the question he knew exactly what would ease his pain.

He wanted her.

Chapter Five

A time for regrets...

Leah knew that look. She'd seen it many times when they were teenagers. The dark depths simmered with passion. Her knees went weak and her body melted into a form that he could mold any way he wanted. He'd always had that effect on her and, sadly, to her dismay, today was no different.

Step away. Step away, she kept repeating to herself. But her feet wouldn't move. All she could see was the warm darkness of his eyes. It had been so long and...

He reached out and circled her neck with his hand, his thumb stroking her jawline. A shiver of excitement ran through her. She tried to squelch it, but failed. With his other hand he pushed her hair away from her face and saw the telltale scar along her scalp line and the bare spot where hair wouldn't grow anymore. He kissed it gently and all the emotions she'd been holding in check exploded inside her. Refusing or stepping away wasn't an option anymore. She hated herself for being weak.

He rained kisses from the scar to her jaw to the hollow of her neck. She breathed in his musky masculine scent and closed her eyes as old feelings took control.

His strength was one of the things she loved about him and she felt it today in every muscle of his body. He captured her lips with an urgency that she remembered well and pulled her against his body. She responded with an aching need and her arms slipped up around his neck. Nothing was said for a while as they remembered a time when two teenagers had found love. A soft moan left her throat as she opened her mouth to give him full access and the world spun away just enough so they could let go.

His hand found the zipper on the back of her dress and slid it down effortlessly. He stroked her skin with mind-numbing caresses until she could no longer think. Nor did she want to. With the twist of his fingers her bra came undone and there was no turning back. He lifted her into his arms and carried her into the bedroom. Neither spoke. They communicated through touches, caresses and kisses.

Her dress had fallen to a pool around her feet. As he laid her on the bed she kicked it away, along with her heels. Somewhere in the haste he removed his clothes. His boots took forever, but she patiently waited. Soon he joined her on the bed and a renewed dance of old began.

His shoulders were broad and strong and capable of transporting her to the moon and back. She ran her fingers through his thick hair and down the rippling muscles of his back. She couldn't seem to touch him enough to feel the power within him. He rolled onto her and she welcomed him with kisses and sighs of delight. It was as if they hadn't forgotten a thing about each other, including ways to please to bring the most satisfaction. But her reaction to his body was somehow stronger, so much more mature and she knew she would never forget this moment when they'd loved as adults.

She cried his name as she reached the pinnacle of complete release and she gripped him tightly as he joined her in moans of pleasure. Afterward, he lay atop her, not moving. After a moment, he rolled to the side and the air-conditioning cooled her sweat-bathed body as the full impact of what they'd done hit her.

Falcon moved from the bed and began to dress. She, too, slipped out and grabbed her silky robe from a chair. Tightening the belt around her waist, she realized her hands were shaking. She'd had so many regrets over the years and this was a big one. It was hard to explain, even to herself. But her life depicted stepping-stones of regret to heaven or to hell. She wasn't quite sure which one yet.

Words ran through her mind but none seemed suitable, so she remained silent. Falcon sat on the bed and then pulled on his jeans. He reached for his shirt on the floor and jammed his arms through the holes. He was seething. She could see that from his darkened face. He was feeling regret as much as she was, and there were no words to soothe their bruised egos.

Snapping the buttons on his shirt, he said, "I don't understand how you can love this David and still make love with me like that." He waved his hand toward the bed in an angry gesture.

She waved her hand, as well. "That was sex. It's always been that way between us."

He frowned. "Sex? That's all we had?"

The truth was going to hurt her as much as it hurt him, but she had to say the words. "In our relationship you never gave me choices. You always made the decisions, no matter how I felt. You pressured me into sex, even though I was hesitant."

"Like now?" His voice rose. "I didn't hear anyone saying stop and I didn't feel you pushing me away. And I never heard the name David."

"This was different."

"You're damn right it was. It was wrong. But…sometimes you drive me crazy. You come back here and expect me to accept everything with a smiling face and a congenial attitude. I'm not built that way. Sorry… Okay, I'll admit I pushed you, but it was what we both wanted."

"In the beginning it made me uncomfortable, and you didn't understand that."

He paled. She'd never seen that before. It shook her, and she tightened the belt on her robe a little more just for something to do.

He ran his hands up his face in a defeated gesture. "I pushed you because I was crazy about you and I thought you felt the same way about me."

"I did," she hastened to reassure him. "But I wanted to wait. And then I got pregnant and you said we had to get married. You never gave me a choice."

"You didn't want to get married?"

"I wanted to talk about it and go over our options. I wanted to be a part of it, not told what to do. Like being told we had to live with your family. That was hard for me. Your brothers were always gawking at me and I felt shy and embarrassed. But I did what you wanted because you were always the dominant one in our relationship."

He shoved his shirt into his jeans. "I did what I thought was best for us at the time, and I see now that it wasn't. But I loved you more than you ever loved me— or maybe you didn't love me at all."

"How many times did you say you loved me?"

"What?" He seemed confused. "Maybe I didn't say it enough, but I showed you every day."

She brushed her hair from her face, trying to say words that wouldn't hurt him. "I did love you, but I was young and unsure of myself and so very confused and conflicted about my life. And then my dad died while I was pregnant and that shook me even more. I was hurting and you never seemed to notice that."

"If you remember, you shut me out. You didn't want me to touch you or anything."

"I didn't want to have sex. That's different."

A twinge nudged his conscience. "Clearly, everything I did was wrong."

She shook her head. "No. It was me, too. I failed to make you understand how I felt, especially after Dad died. I wanted to move in with my aunt so we'd have more privacy, but you wouldn't listen to me. You kept saying you were going to clean out your parents' old house for us."

"Leah, I didn't have time. I had to be up at five and on the ranch working. I had a baby on the way and had to make a living for us. And living in town was out of the question."

She blinked away an errant tear. "I just felt like I didn't have any choices. I…I felt trapped. We were two teenagers having to live with our mistakes, but I never really saw Eden as a mistake. I just couldn't deal with all that responsibility, I suppose. I was weak and that's all on me."

"It may surprise you to know that I now know exactly how you felt back then because Eden is feeling the same way now. We talked about it last night."

"Oh."

"A boy is pressuring her to have sex and she's not ready."

"She talks to you about things like that?"

"Eden and I talk about everything. I made a point of being honest with her and telling her the truth when she was small, especially after Dad died and I had to explain about death. Not having a mother drew us closer."

Leah let the last part slide. She wasn't ready to open that wound again. "What did you tell her?"

"She asked if I had pressured you to have sex and I told her the truth, that I had."

"How did she respond to that?"

"It made her unsure about love because she sees us as having a great love affair."

Leah looked down at her bare feet, not daring to look at Falcon, afraid that her feelings would show in her eyes. "I guess all kids want to believe that."

"Yeah." He sat on the bed and yanked on his boots. "I learned more today than I really wanted to about our relationship, but I think it's time to close those doors to the past. We were two teenagers and, yes, I took control and gave you very few choices. I'm sorry about that, but I was young trying to do the right thing. Evidently, it was wrong and I can admit that now." He stood in one easy movement. "So you can have your divorce to marry someone that you love. You deserve that, and that's not easy for me to say."

She swallowed the lump in her throat. "Thank you. I…I don't know what to say."

"Don't say anything. Sometimes when we look back on our lives all we see are the regrets and the things we didn't do. But when I look back at us I see two teenagers deeply in love, and I will keep that memory just as it is in my mind because it gave me Eden."

Tears clogged her throat and she couldn't speak. She didn't expect him to be so gracious. He certainly had changed in more ways than she could've ever imagined. Or maybe the young Leah never really saw him, just the handsome cowboy she wanted to notice her, to love her.

He moved for the door. "Just send me the papers. I'll talk to Eden and let you know what she says about meeting you. If she doesn't want to, I can't make her. It's just that simple."

"I understand."

"I wish *I* did. I'm really trying, but I'll never believe that you didn't love me with all your heart back then." He walked out of the bedroom. Tears began to roll from her eyes, and she made no move to brush them away. She heard the click of the door as he left and that's when she became a blubbering idiot. She sank onto the bed, a total mess.

"I did and I still love you, but it's better you never know that," she mumbled through her tears.

FALCON DROVE TO the barn, angry at himself, angry at the world and angry that life could be so cruel. He should have met her in a public place, not a hotel room. That was only asking for trouble because she was right when she said that it had always been very passionate between them. That's why her saying he pushed her more than she wanted really crushed him. He had thought they loved each other and that's what people in love did, especially as an eighteen-year-old boy. Now he had to live with what he'd done today. Another regret among the many that crowded the shadows of his soul.

In this, Eden was most important. He had to make sure she was not hurt. He, on the other hand, had broad shoulders and could take it. That's what he kept telling himself as he saddled Titan.

"Hey, you're back," Quincy said as he walked into the barn.

Falcon cinched the saddle a little tighter. "Why aren't you with the roundup crew?"

"Elias broke the tag gun so I came back to get another."

Falcon continued to work with the saddle, not in a mood to talk.

"Are you okay? It's not like you to miss the beginning of roundup."

"Egan knows the cows as well as I do and he knows how to cull the herd. Jude, too. And they have a good eye for saving heifers and bulls."

"Yeah, but we're used to you giving orders."

Falcon turned to stare at his brother. "Are you saying I'm controlling and dominating?"

Quincy held up his hands. "Whoa. Where's that coming from? After Dad died and you took over, we accepted that because we needed someone to be boss. If not, we'd be arguing all the time. You've never minded before when we've teased you, so what's up now?"

He was feeling a little bruised by what Leah had said. But he was a leader and that meant being controlling. It wasn't easy to corral six brothers and have them do their jobs the like were supposed to. It was different between a man and wife, though, and he should've been more receptive to Leah's feelings. He hadn't been and that's why his ego had taken a hit. Having a daughter had changed him over the years. But he'd failed Leah so badly he was never going to lose that bruised feeling.

Quincy was waiting for an answer and Falcon had just drifted off to another place. That was so not like him, and by the frown on Quincy's face he knew Quincy was thinking the same thing. He and Quincy were more than brothers. They were best friends. And he had to tell someone, because they all had to know Leah was back.

"I saw someone from the past this morning and it was jarring, reminded me of my faults and my weaknesses. It wasn't a pretty picture and I'm still feeling conflicted."

"Who was it?"

Falcon exhaled a deep breath. "Leah."

"What? She's back?"

"Yeah."

"What did she want? Where has she been?"

"She wants to see Eden."

"Are you going to allow it?"

Falcon shrugged. "Eden will be eighteen in January and I'm going to let her make that decision because I don't want her to hate me later for keeping her away from her mother."

"Oh, man, I can't believe she just came back like that."

"It's a long story." Falcon told Quincy everything Leah had told him and Quincy's eyes opened wide as Falcon talked.

"Is she okay now?"

"She's as beautiful as ever."

Quincy's eyes narrowed. "Are you sure she's telling the truth?"

"Yeah. I saw the scars." *And touched them, too.*

His brother eyed him. Falcon didn't want him to

see too much. His time with Leah was private and he wouldn't share that with anyone.

"I'll tell the family later today, so keep it under your hat."

"No problem. Are you sure you're okay?"

Falcon put his boot in the stirrup. "No. I haven't been since the day she left." He kneed Titan and rode out of the barn.

And he wasn't ever likely to be again.

ROUNDUP KEPT FALCON busy and he didn't have time to think about what had happened today. It was late afternoon by the time they rode back into the barn. Some were in trucks pulling trailers. They'd culled several older cows that would go to the auction barn. Tomorrow they would start all over again.

Everyone was unsaddling, finishing up for the day and eager to go their various ways. Egan was always the first one through, as he was today, and he headed toward the door.

"I'm going to the house to fix supper for anyone who wants to eat," his mother said, also heading for the door.

"Egan, Mom, could you wait a minute? I'd like to talk to everyone."

Jericho quickly made his exit toward a back door and Falcon saw him. "You, too, Jericho. You're not only Egan's friend, you're part of the family now."

Jericho strolled back in and leaned against a post. The man had more than proved himself and his loyalty to the Rebel family. Falcon trusted him completely.

The rest of the family gathered around, most of them sinking onto bales of hay, including Grandpa, who was never far away.

"Come on, Falcon." Paxton sat by Grandpa. "We're tired and you don't have anything to complain about today. We worked our butts off, and I had a rope on the cow that tried to get away in a heartbeat."

"Yeah," Phoenix spoke up. "On the second try."

"Shut up."

Phoenix danced in front of his brother with his fists in the air. "Make me."

"Stop it. I'm not in a mood for this today."

Phoenix stopped dancing and stared at his brother, as did everyone, and their mother walked closer to Falcon. "What is it, son?"

He didn't know how else to say it except to just say the words out loud. "I saw Leah today."

Complete silence filled the barn. Even the old tomcat stilled on the rafters.

"Well, I'll be damned." Grandpa was first to speak. "They say bad pennies always turn up."

"What did she want?" his mother asked.

"She wants to see Eden."

"No way," Elias said. "There's no way any of us will allow her anywhere near Cupcake." His brothers had always called Eden Cupcake. They probably needed to change that now since she was older, but it was just second nature to them.

"It's Eden's choice, not ours." Falcon made that clear in a voice they understood.

"Where has she been?" Paxton wanted to know.

Once again Falcon told the story and again there was silence.

"That's terrible," his mother said. "And just so sad. How is she now?"

"She seems fine." He didn't make the mistake of saying she was beautiful again. "I got the feeling she just wants to get on with her life now."

"With someone else." Elias grunted. "That's rich."

"I'm through judging Leah," Falcon said. "I'd appreciate it if all of you would stay out of it. Right now, my concern is my daughter, and I will do everything to protect her."

"She's not taking Cupcake." Grandpa made his views clear.

"She just wants to see her, Grandpa. That's it."

"Nah." Grandpa shook his head. "Something else is going on here. You better be on your toes, boy."

"I'm always on my toes."

"Yeah. And we'll be right beside you."

"Just tell us what you want us to do," Egan said.

"Be there for Eden if she wants to talk and don't say anything bad about her mother. That's my bottom line. She has to make up her own mind about Leah so don't share your viewpoint."

"You got it," echoed around the barn.

"Thanks. Now I have to talk to my daughter."

"She's practicing with Dancer in my corral," Quincy told him.

On his way to Quincy's paint horse operation, which was about a hundred yards from the main barn, he kept going over and over in his head what he was going to say. He didn't have a set script. He would go with the truth and be as honest as possible with his daughter. And just maybe they could get through this.

Chapter Six

A time for mothers and daughters...

John Rebel had stipulated in his will that each son would receive one-seventh of the ranch, but only after their mother's death. She would be in complete control until then or until she decided otherwise. Quincy had already staked out the part he wanted and everyone had agreed to it. It was still a part of Rebel Ranch, but eventually it would be Quincy's.

He'd built a barn and corrals for his paints and his off time was spent there. Large live oaks, at least one hundred years old, shaded a lot of it. A perfect place for a home. Quincy was thinking ahead, Falcon was always in the present looking back. Today, some of that would change.

Eden was astride a brown-and-white paint and Zane sat on a post with a stopwatch. At Zane's signal Eden shot out of the barn and made the cloverleaf pattern around the barrels Quincy had set up. Falcon leaned on the fence, watching his daughter. Her long dark hair flew behind her as she kneed the horse faster to get the best time.

She was probably the best rider on the ranch. She'd

been in the saddle since she was three months old and she moved with the horse, which was breathtaking to watch. His daughter was beautiful—just like her mother. Horse and rider shot into the barn and Zane clicked the watch. Eden slowly trotted Dancer out.

"What was it?" she asked Zane.

"Fifteen seconds."

"I can do better than that. Let's go again."

"Zane," Jude called. "We have to go to school to talk to your teacher again."

"Aw, Dad."

"I'm not the one falling asleep in class because I'm bored."

Zane jumped off the post. "I know all that stuff and it's boring to go over it again and again."

"That's what we're going to talk about."

Zane was smart like his mother and he would probably go off to a prestigious college in a few years, as his mother had. Falcon hoped Zane made better choices than Paige. But then, everyone had to make their own choices and live with them. That's what he was trying to do now.

"You time me, Dad," Eden said as Jude and Zane walked off.

"We need to talk."

Dancer pranced around and Eden kept pace with her. "Can we do it later? I'm getting faster and faster. Did you see?"

"Yeah. You're doing great, but this is important. You can practice tomorrow. You have homework."

"Dad, I'm seventeen. You don't have to tell me these things anymore."

He probably didn't, but he'd hang on just as long as he could. "Unsaddle Dancer. I'll wait."

She must've sensed the urgency in his voice because she complied without an argument. He followed her into the barn and she tended to the horse. He taught her that a long time ago, but it seemed like yesterday when she would say, "Daddy, I can do it. I can do it," when she could barely reach the horse.

He eased onto some bales of alfalfa Quincy had stacked near the door. He didn't want his baby to be hurt but there was no way to stop that. No matter what happened next, Eden was going to be hurt.

With her jeans tucked into her boots, she walked toward him. She'd worn her jeans like that as long as he could remember. She plopped down beside him.

"What's up? You have a big frowny face."

He wouldn't argue that. Of all the talks he'd had with his daughter over the years this one would be the hardest.

He leaned forward, his elbows on his knees. "Something has happened and you need to know about it."

"Is Grandpa sick again?" Grandpa had had the flu last winter and Eden, afraid he was going to die, had waited on him hand and foot. His daughter had a very big heart.

"No, Grandpa is his cantankerous self."

"Is it Grandma?"

He had to stop the guessing game. "No. It's about your mother."

"What?"

Hearing a tremor in her voice, he turned to her. "She's back."

Her eyes opened wide. "You mean here…in Horseshoe?"

"Yes."

Eden jumped up, her eyes blazing. "Why now? What does she want?"

"She wants to see you."

"Fat chance. As far as I'm concerned, I don't have a mother. And how come you're not angry? You're so calm."

Falcon studied the tips of his boots covered in dust. "When she called, I was angry. Very angry. So I wanted answers before I would talk to her. She had to tell me where she'd been and what she'd been doing all these years and she had to explain why she'd left so suddenly."

"Did she?"

"Yes, and it wasn't what I'd expected. It was a bit terrifying to know what she'd been through."

Eden sat by him again, a little closer as if she needed his support. Again, he told the story as Leah had told him.

Eden rested her head on his shoulder. "That's so sad. But if she's better, why has it taken her so long to come home?"

As much as he hated to, he had to be honest with his daughter so he told her about David and the Thornwall family.

"She found another family and forgot about us."

Falcon wrapped his arm around his daughter. "I don't think she forgot about us. She was just afraid to come home and—" he took a deep breath "—she found someone to love her the way she wanted."

Eden jumped up again. "Why has she come back at all, then? It just makes it hurt that much more."

"I know, baby, and I can't explain it. All I know is your mother wants to see you for a few minutes."

Eden shook her head. "No. I don't want to see her. If she can't stay, I'd just as soon she stayed away."

Falcon didn't want to push her, but he had to make her understand something. "It's your decision. This might be your only chance to see her or meet her. Think about that. You have a right to confront her and tell her how you're feeling. You're old enough to understand that."

"You're not angry with her anymore?"

"No, but I'm not happy about what she's doing. It's her choice, though, and I have to respect that. She wants to move on and as much as I want her to give us a chance I can't make her do that, so I'll give her the divorce that she wants. We all need to move on."

"I wish you were yelling or something because when you're calm like this it gives me the heebie-jeebies."

He got to his feet. "It wasn't easy to see your mother, but I've worried about her for years. I finally lost all that worry and I just want to put all this behind me. Above all the angst, I want you to be able to deal with this like an adult and I'll be right there beside you whatever you decide."

Eden raised her head, her back straight. "I'm a Rebel, my father's daughter, and I can handle seeing my mother. So tell her yes, I will meet her, but only here at Rebel Ranch with you beside me. I'm not saying I'll be nice and cordial. I'm just saying I'll meet her."

He hugged her. "I'm proud of you, baby girl."

Arm in arm they walked toward the house and Falcon prayed that everything went smoothly with Leah. Whatever happened, he had to pick up the pieces and move on for his daughter.

LEAH GOT FALCON'S call at about six and she was out the door in a few minutes. She was going to see her baby, or, more to the point, her grown-up daughter. David said she could do it, but her nerves were jumpy and her head ached. She just wanted to get through this to be able to face the future without all of the turmoil inside her. She wasn't sure that was going to happen. It was a start, though.

She was hoping Eden would come to the hotel, but Falcon had said that was out of the question. There was no room to bargain because this was her last chance and she took it. Facing Kate Rebel would be hard, but she could get through that, too. She and her mother-in-law had never gotten along. Looking back, Leah really never gave her a chance. Just as she'd never given her marriage a chance. She had so much to deal with as a teenager and she wasn't equipped to handle any of it. Now she had to be a mature adult and face what she'd done and say, "I'm sorry." She could do that. She could do a lot of things, but she didn't know if she could take her daughter's hatred. The hour ahead loomed darkly and she wanted to turn around and go back to Houston. She didn't.

As she drove, she thought about what had happened that morning. Such a mistake. She guessed a person never got too old to make them. Putting the past behind her didn't start with having sex with her husband. In response, she had lashed out at Falcon about the past and she'd never meant to do that. She would have to say another "I'm sorry" before she left for the last time.

Driving over the Rebel Ranch cattle guard, her nerves tingled. She hoped there would be only her, Falcon and Eden. She wasn't sure how many of the other brothers were married or still living around the ranch. It was none of her business. She had to concentrate on what was ahead. She parked in front of the house, drew a deep breath, got out and walked to the big pine front doors and knocked tentatively.

Falcon let her in. His face was creased with worry, but she couldn't turn back now. Her daughter awaited.

"Be prepared for some attitude," he said.

"I never thought for a minute this would be easy."

"Then let's go into the den." She wanted to reach for his arm and ask for something but she didn't know what. All she knew was that she needed his support. She swallowed hard and followed him. Eden stood by a big stone fireplace in jeans and boots, her long hair hanging down her back. Leah didn't have time to look around, but there didn't seem to be anyone else in the room. She only focused on the young girl who was glaring at her.

"This is your mother, Leah," Falcon said to Eden and stood next to their daughter.

A rush of nerves assailed Leah and she had trouble breathing, but she stared straight into her daughter's green eyes, so like her own. "It's nice to meet you. I've thought about you so much over the years and not a day has gone by that I didn't pray that you were well and being taken care of by your father."

"My father has always been here for me." Eden almost spat the words. "I know that I can count on him for anything. When I think of him, I feel this big hug around my heart. When I think if you, all I feel is anger that you could leave a little baby."

Leah swallowed the sob in her throat and words eluded her. This was Eden's moment and she had a right to say whatever she wanted. But the pain was sharper than Leah had expected.

"Dad told me about your mother and the accident and everything that happened to you. I don't know how to respond to that because all I know is I lost my mother and I don't think there's any way to get her back now."

Leah found her voice. "Your father did a great job raising you."

"That's because he's a great person."

"I know that."

Eden flipped back her hair. "Then why come back if you don't want to stay?"

Leah fought for words. "I don't live in Horseshoe anymore. My life is in Houston. You may not understand, but I've waited so long to make this decision and it's time for me to start a new life. I can't do that until I tell you how sorry I am about what happened. If I could go back, I would change everything. I would talk to your father and tell him what I was feeling so he could help me. I know now that he would have. But I made all the wrong choices and now I have to live with that. You're my child and I will always love you. You don't have to love me back. I lost that right a long time ago."

Eden was silent for a moment, but Leah sensed a chink in her armor of defiance. "You really love this other guy?"

Leah choked back another sob. "He took care of me when I needed someone and we became very close. Yes, I love him."

"Then why come back? You should've stayed away."

Leah's head throbbed and she touched her forehead. *Not now.* She needed just a few more minutes. The room began to sway and she knew she wasn't going to get those minutes. "Oh." She tried to remain focused, but she felt herself falling, falling until everything was black for a second. She crumpled to the floor.

"Daddy, what's wrong with her?" Eden's question pierced the blackness.

"Calm down, baby. She's just nervous." Then two strong arms lifted her onto the sofa and Falcon's callused hands smoothed her cheeks. "Leah, are you all right?"

Everything was coming into focus and she could see his handsome face, the worry lines.

"I…"

"Get a glass of water," he told Eden.

Leah slowly sat up and brushed her hair from her face. "I'm sorry. My nerves are getting the best of me."

"Take a couple of deep breaths."

Eden came back with a glass of water and handed it to her. She clasped it like a lifeline, needing to hold something. After a couple of moments, she said, "I really have to go." She stood with as much dignity as possible."

Falcon stood beside her. "Are you sure you're okay?"

"Yes." Her eyes settled on Eden's startled face. She was so beautiful it took Leah's breath away. So young, with her whole life ahead of her. Leah hoped she hadn't done anything that would leave bad feelings for the future. "Thank you for allowing me to come. You're just as I pictured you in my dreams." Eden just stared at her and Leah knew she should go, but she held back. "Do you mind if I hug you?"

"Uh…"

At Eden's hesitation, Leah backed off. "It's okay."

Eden glanced at her father and then said, "I don't mind."

Leah's heart beat so fast she could barely move, but she took a step toward her daughter and wrapped her arms around her. She held and hugged her as if it was for the last time because it was. When she was about to draw away, Eden's arms went around Leah's waist and she hugged her back. Tears stung the back of Leah's eyes. She didn't hope for this much. She felt blessed.

She took a step backward. "Thank you and goodbye." She turned toward the door, unable to endure any more. Falcon was right behind her and followed her to the car.

"Thank you," was all she could say. Her hands shook and she gripped the car door for support.

"I don't understand what you're doing, but I'm not going to question you. I just wish you'd call your daughter every now and then just to let her know you care."

Leah bit her lip. "I'll think about it."

He shook his head, but didn't say anything.

"I'm sorry I was so critical this morning. I was just upset that I was so weak and allowed my basic instincts to take over. You did nothing wrong in our marriage. You did everything right. I'm the one to blame." She gripped the door a little tighter. "You were right, as always. We were deeply in love, but I was too young to know what I had or wise enough to accept it. Eden was conceived in love and I want her to know that. I hope someday you can forgive me for all the pain I've caused you."

"Think about including her in your life. It would mean so much. She needs a mother now more than ever."

Dusk had settled in and the wind chilled her heated skin—or was it yesterday's memories clamped around her heart? Falcon wanted the impossible. She'd come back because she had to see her baby and she didn't know how to explain that any other way. She couldn't tell him everything. It was best to go.

"I…" Words failed her again. There was nothing she could say that would soothe his bruised ego.

He must've sensed her objection. "So this is the final goodbye?"

"Yes. It has to be and it hurts me just as much as it's hurting you and Eden. Please believe that."

"Are you going to tell David what happened this morning between us?"

"Of course. We have an honest and open relationship."

"Really? The man must be very understanding."

"He is. He won't be happy, but we'll work through it. That's what couples do, as I've learned the hard way. I'll send you the divorce papers."

"Then it will really be over," he said in a somber voice. "But from what I felt this morning it's far from over. You're being very mysterious about this whole thing and I feel something else is going on here."

"Goodbye, Falcon. Take care of our daughter. I'll never forget you." She got in the car and drove away, refusing to look back at everything she was losing. At everything she never had. And at everything that could never be. Tears rolled from her eyes and she kept driving.

It was over. She'd done what she'd set out to do and now she could face her uncertain future.

Chapter Seven

A time to face consequences...

Falcon watched until Leah's car disappeared out of sight. She was gone as quickly as she had come back into his life. He had to go forward this time, knowing that their relationship was really over. Before, he'd always wondered and worried about her. Now he knew she was okay and living in Houston and planning a life with someone else. He wasn't afraid to admit how much that stung. That morning proved how weak he was when it came to Leah.

One minute he was angry and the next he was loving her like he'd never loved before. And she hadn't protested. That's what bothered him. If she really loved the other guy, how could she make such passionate love with him? He'd probably never know the answer, and he had to move on for himself and their daughter. Eden wasn't handling this well.

In the den, his daughter was curled up in the corner of the sofa, tears rolling down her cheeks.

He sat beside her. "Hey, baby girl, why all the tears?"

Eden curled into his side. "I...I want her to stay, but she won't. How can she leave us again?"

He wrapped his arms around his sad baby. "I don't think it was easy for her, either. I'm not taking up for her or anything, but she made a decision to start a new life and she couldn't until she had closure on her past or whatever she's calling it."

"But…"

He kissed the top of her head. "You don't seem angry anymore, just hurt."

"She seems so sad and when she fainted, I felt terrible for saying those things to her. Do you think she's ill or something?"

"I think she was just nervous."

"Yeah." Eden became quiet, and then she asked, "Dad, do you think she'd mind if I called her sometime and went to Houston and had lunch with her like mothers and daughters do?"

Falcon hated to crush her hopes, but he felt there was no place for Eden in Leah's life and he had to prepare her. "Baby, why don't we let go and move on like she wants us to? This was goodbye and we have to respect her wishes."

Eden sat up with a fire in her eyes that Falcon knew well. "Well, I'll be eighteen soon and I can do what I want. And I just might want to go to Houston to see my mother. If she doesn't like that, then she can tell me to my face."

"Oh, Lord, help us all," Falcon said as he got to his feet.

"I can, Dad."

"I know, but give it some time. Now, Mom is making patty melts at Quincy's so let's go have supper."

Arm in arm they walked toward the back door. "I've decided I don't love Brandon, Dad."

He was taken aback for a moment because Brandon

was the last thing on his mind. "That seems very sudden. How did you come to that conclusion?"

"Because I don't look at him the way you looked at my mother."

His heart skipped a beat. Was he that obvious? "How is that?" he asked, trying for nonchalance.

"With moonbeams in your eyes."

He stopped walking and stared at his daughter. "Eden, that's silly. I don't look at your mother that way."

She tilted her head in a sly manner. "Oh, Dad, you lie. Moonbeams were shooting all over the den because you weren't the only one with them in your eyes. She had them, too. There's a lot of fire still there and, you know, she's not married yet and I bet you're ten times better than this David."

He shook his head. "Why do women always weave these fantasies?"

"Because there would be no babies if we didn't."

He tried not to smile and failed. "Baby, please accept that there is no future for me and your mother. That's only asking for a heartache."

"Maybe. Maybe not."

They went out the back door and Falcon tried hard not to get caught up in Eden's fantasy, but after what had happened this morning he was already feeling the heartache. And wondering why there wasn't a future for them when they had so much passion. But, as he'd told Eden, he had to let go. It would be his greatest test of strength.

LEAH TREMBLED SEVERELY and her vision was blurred. She was forced to pull over to the side of the road. Resting her head on the steering wheel, she took several deep breaths and then looked up. Everything was still blurry and fear shot through her. *Not now.* She reached for her purse on the passenger seat and pulled out her phone.

She could barely make out the icons on the screen. David answered immediately.

"David, I'm scared. I'm trembling and my vision is blurred."

"Where are you?"

"On Rebel Road."

"So you've seen them?"

"Yes, and I shouldn't have come. It was selfish and you should've stopped me."

"You've been trying to do this for years, Leah. It was time."

"We'll talk about that later, but right now I need to get off this road before Falcon or any of the family sees me."

"Do you have your pills and some water?"

"Yes."

"Take one."

"I took one this morning."

"It won't hurt to take another."

"Okay. Wait a minute." She fished her medication out of her purse and found a bottle of water in the console. "I've taken it, but my vision is still blurred."

"Lean back your head and breathe deeply. Calm down. I think this is the result of the trauma of seeing your husband and your daughter after so many years."

"It was wonderful and awful at the same time. They were nicer than they should have been."

"Don't say that. You were dealt a hard blow, Leah. None of it was your fault."

"I ran away like a scared little girl."

"Leah...why don't I come and get you? You need

someone, and I don't like you driving if you're not feeling well."

Leah opened her eyes and she could see. Relief washed over her. "No, don't. I'm better. Really. My vision is back. I'll just drive to the hotel and stay another night. I'll come home in the morning. I don't feel right driving all the way to Houston in this condition, either."

"Are you sure? I can get Callie to come with me to drive your car."

"No, don't bother Callie. She's busy at college and I'm fine now." Callie was David's daughter and in her first year at Rice University.

"From your reaction, I'm guessing you didn't tell them the truth."

Leah's stomach cramped. "No. I couldn't do that, but I had to see them and that's the part that was selfish. I should've thought about them more."

"If you would just tell them, it would be so much easier on you and them."

"Then what? I refuse to be a burden to them."

"Leah, that's life. Families rally together in times of trouble and I'm sure your husband would appreciate the honesty."

She took another deep breath. "I've made a decision and I'm sticking to it. I've made all the arrangements and I'm not changing anything now. That's the way I want it."

"You know I love you, but sometimes you don't make much sense."

"I've made so many bad decisions, but I feel this one is right for all of us. I got to see and hold my daughter. She let me hug her and I feel so grateful for that. Now I can do what I have to."

"I'll support you like I always have, but I firmly believe that Falcon deserves to know and so does your daughter."

"David, please…"

"You made a mistake, Leah. But you were so young and you paid dearly for it in the years that followed. Just tell Falcon. I feel sure he would understand."

Yes, Falcon was more understanding than she ever thought possible. She thought about telling him about her condition so many times, but all she could think about was Falcon having to take care of her and watch the misery that she would have to go through. She couldn't do that to him. He deserved better. They had no future and there was no need to lead him on. The morning was a sweet agony she would remember to her last day. It was the perfect way to say goodbye.

"Do you think you can drive down tomorrow?" David's voice pierced her thoughts.

"Yes. I'll call you before I leave."

"You call me when you reach the hotel tonight."

"You're such a worrywart."

David laughed and Leah clicked off. Staring straight ahead, she started the engine and pulled out onto the lonely country road. The urge to go back and be honest with Falcon plagued her, but she knew she was doing the right thing. She couldn't heap all her troubles onto his shoulders after what she'd done to him. She had to go this journey alone.

THE NEXT MORNING Leah was better, so she headed for Houston. Miss Hattie's house, a large, brown, brick two-story with a pool, was in Bellaire. It was close to the medical center, as Miss Hattie's husband had been a doctor. Life had dealt her some cruel blows but Miss Hattie was a blessing she would always be grateful for.

As she opened the back door, she heard music. Leah smiled. She'd given Alma, the housekeeper, time off while she was away, but evidently she was back.

"Alma!" she called, placing her suitcase on the floor.

The music stopped and Alma appeared from the living area with a hand over her heart. "My goodness, Miss Leah, you scared the dickens out of me."

Leah picked up the mail on the desk by the door. "What are you doing here? You didn't enjoy your time off?"

Alma wiped her hands on an oversize print apron. "Mr. David called and said you were coming home and you might need me."

"He worries too much."

Alma shook a finger at her. "And you're too stubborn." The woman gave her a narrow-eyed gaze. "You're pale. Go sit down and I'll fix you some chamomile tea."

Leah obediently went because she was feeling drained and alone. For years she'd dreamed of seeing Falcon and Eden again and now that she had, there didn't seem to be any reason to keep fighting, to keep going. Her defeatist attitude was getting the better of her and she would get her emotions under control in a minute. But first, she wanted to be sad. Sometimes a woman just had to feel sad.

Voices penetrated her gloom and soon David appeared in the living room.

"You made it," he said, lowering his tall, lean form to sit on the sofa beside her. He must have hurried over because his grayish-blond hair was still damp from the shower. "You don't look good."

"Thank you."

He picked up her wrist and took her pulse. "It's a little high. I'm worried about you. This trip was too much."

Leah leaned her head back on the sofa. "In so many ways it was, but in others it was just what I needed."

"I've made an appointment with Dr. Morris for nine tomorrow morning. You need to see him so he can determine if we need to move the surgery forward."

"I'm fine. I just need to rest. And shouldn't you be in the office?"

"I don't see my first patient until one."

"But you have patients at the hospital you need to see."

"Family comes first," he told her.

The sentiment gave her the warm fuzzies. "I wish Miss Hattie was here."

"She would be fussing over you."

"I know. I never had a real mom and Miss Hattie was everything a mother should be. She taught me so much and I still miss her."

David patted her knee. "That's very generous of you, considering she caused you so much misery."

"Mmm. Like I told her so many times, I shouldn't have run across the intersection on a yellow light. She didn't mean to hurt me, like…"

"Like what?"

"Like I didn't mean to hurt Falcon and Eden."

"Leah."

"I know some people don't understand that, but Miss Hattie and I made a connection that transcended blame." She tucked her bare feet beneath her. "Let's talk about something else. You're not going to be pleased when I tell you what I did."

He smiled slightly. "I'm sure it was heinous."

"I used you shamelessly."

"How?"

"I told Falcon we were in love and planning to get married and that's why I wanted a divorce."

"Why would you do that?"

She shifted restlessly. "Because Falcon is a responsible, take-control kind of guy and if I told him the truth, he'd take over my life—and he doesn't deserve to be saddled with me now."

"Leah…"

"I needed a scapegoat and you were the only one available."

"And he believed you?"

She shrugged. "I didn't give him a choice."

"I know you did what you had to—or what you felt you had to. I just wish you would let them into your life."

She shook her head. "Please, let's don't do this again. In a little over three weeks, they will remove the tumor from my brain and it will either be successful or I will have complications. I could lose my sight. There are always risks, Dr. Morris said, and I will not put Falcon or Eden through that."

"You keep forgetting there is a slim chance that you will be fine. Dr. Morris is an exceptional surgeon or I would have never sent you to him. I have faith he can remove the tumor without debilitating results."

"But he also said it keeps growing and he's not sure if he can remove it completely without side effects. He was quite honest about that."

"Doctors have to be honest when surgery is this dangerous." He patted her knee again. "I'll be right there with you and so will the family."

She looked straight at him. "And you will follow my directive?"

"Yes. You will not be put on life support and I will keep my word about not notifying Falcon and Eden until…"

His words trailed off and Leah had a catch in her throat, but she didn't waver in her decision. "Yes."

"How do you think he's going to feel when he gets that call?"

"David, please." She glanced to the white orchid growing on a side table. Miss Hattie had loved orchids. It was easier to think of the good times instead of the bad.

"After all you've been through, I get so angry when I think about what has been done to your life."

There was silence for a moment because Leah had no words. Life was what it was and she had to continue until the very end.

She brushed hair from her face. "Let me tell you about Eden. She's so beautiful and spunky. Falcon did a great job raising her and I was surprised to learn he took charge of that instead of his mother."

"Why are you surprised?"

"Because he's the strong alpha male and someone I mistakenly thought wanted the woman in the home raising the baby and doing housework. I was so wrong. He took Eden with him on horseback when he worked on the ranch. He said since she didn't have a mother he wanted to make sure she knew that she was loved by her father."

"Did that hurt?"

"You bet it did, but I was just overwhelmed by the man Falcon is now. He's loving, caring and compassionate. I guess I knew he had those qualities, but I only saw him as a person in control."

"Over you?"

She sighed. "I guess it made me realize I never really gave him or our marriage a chance. I was just so scared of doing all the wrong things and in the end I did the worst thing possible."

"Everyone makes mistakes, Leah, and one of these days you need to forgive yourself. I hope it's soon for your sake."

She smiled at him. "You really should have been a psychiatrist."

"Maybe. But there was something mystical about the young girl my mother hit on that rainy day. No name, no identification. Nothing. We all felt so bad for you and we prayed and hoped you would make it. It was touch and go for so long but we stood by you because you touched our hearts just by your presence."

"It seems like a lifetime ago."

"Now you have another hurdle to get through. You have to survive so you can return to your family, the ones who love you, and the ones who have been waiting for you."

She reached over and hugged him. "I don't know how I got so lucky to know people like you and your family. I can face the future because of y'all."

"But you need your real family," he stated clearly.

"David, please stop pressuring me."

He stood and kissed her forehead. "Get some rest and remember the appointment tomorrow. Now I have to break the news to my wife that I'm getting married."

Leah laughed. "I'll explain to Anne."

"Don't worry. She'll waddle over here sometime this afternoon."

Anne and David lived three blocks away. They had

two daughters, Callie and Calise, who were nineteen and seventeen, and they were expecting their third child— their surprise baby. Since Anne and David were doctors, they were mystified how it had happened. It was the cause of a lot of laughter and happiness in the family.

After David left, Leah drank her tea and then curled up on the sofa and thought about family. Her family. Her real family, as David had said. Memories of Falcon warmed her heart. She would hold him and Eden there and hopefully she would see them again one day. She could only pray for a miracle.

Chapter Eight

A time to move on...

Life went on, as Falcon soon found. The ranch kept him busy, but at the oddest times an image of Leah would slip through. It had been a week now and every day he waited for the divorce papers, but they didn't come. He'd never been divorced so he didn't know how long it would take. But he assumed it would be soon.

Two weeks passed and still no papers. He had Leah's number and he thought of calling, but he wasn't that eager to be divorced, so he kept waiting.

Eden had a rodeo scheduled for the end of September and she was concentrating on that. She hadn't mentioned her mother again and he wondered what she was plotting because he knew her mother was never far from her mind, as was the case with him.

They were finishing the roundup. A cool front had blown through and it wasn't quite so hot. They tagged, vaccinated and branded all the new calves and separated the bigger ones from their mothers to go to auction. There was a lot of bellowing in protest from the mothers. One big steer shot from the herd and headed for the brushy woods. If he made it, they would spend hours trying to find him in the thick bushes.

Quickly, he kneed his horse and reached for his rope looped over the saddle horn. "Header," he called, adjusting the rope, cantering after the calf. "Header, Egan." His brother immediately readied his rope.

Falcon threw his rope and a big loop landed over the steer's head. He jerked it and the calf came to a sudden stop, kicking up dirt. Egan threw his rope at the calf's back legs and caught one in a perfect loop. The calf went down and the horses backed up to hold him tight.

Falcon dismounted and studied the steer's horns that were beginning to grow pointy and sharp. "Quincy, bring the dehorner. Let's get these before they get much bigger."

Within minutes, the steer's horns were gone and they quickly ushered him back to the herd.

Paxton rode up. "Damn, Falcon, that was some nice roping. I couldn't have done it better."

Phoenix laughed.

Paxton shot him a dark look. "Shut up."

"Falcon's a better header than you'll ever be," Phoenix told him.

"Shut up or I'll knock you off that saddle."

"Try it."

"Stop it!" Falcon shouted. "It's been a long day and I'm not listening to any bickering. It's time to load up the portable pens and head back to the ranch. Jericho has already taken the trailer with the calves and now it's time to finish up."

Paxton saluted in a mock gesture. "Yes, sir."

Falcon ignored him. It was just a day in the life of the Rebels. Arguing and fighting was the norm. That's who they were and Falcon wouldn't change them, but some days all the bickering got on his nerves, especially when he had so much on his mind.

He rode into the barn tired and weary, ready for a shower and food. They were all feeling the same way as they unsaddled their horses. Grandpa sat on a hay bale, chewing on a toothpick, watching them.

"Did I ever tell you boys about the time your dad and me did roundup all by ourselves? It was rough, but we got it done."

Falcon inwardly groaned as he threw his saddle over a rail. He didn't want to hear stories about his dad. It hurt too much to realize he wasn't there, but Grandpa kept talking.

"We had this rangy bull with horns. Long horns, and he didn't like being penned up. As John ran him into the pen, that lousy bull turned and ripped a horn right across John's leg. John said a few cuss words that would burn his mama's ears and reached for his rope. He roped that bull and tied him to a post in the pen where he couldn't move. But that bull, he kept fighting, trying to get loose. I got John the dehorner and he snipped those horns right down to the skull, blood gushing from his leg. I knew better than to point that out because my boy was fighting mad. I learned a long time ago to just let him work through it."

Even though he didn't want to, Falcon was listening avidly, as were his brothers.

Elias sat by Grandpa. "What happened next?"

"Well—" Grandpa scratched his scraggly beard "—that's when your mama showed up. Falcon must've been about three. Quincy was toddling around and Kate was pregnant with Egan. She used to pull y'all around in a little red wagon. She told Falcon and Quincy to stay put in the wagon and she went into the barn to get the medical box we kept there. Without saying a word, she went into the pen and tied a red handkerchief around your dad's leg to stop the bleeding. She knew your dad wasn't going to stop until the roundup was finished."

"What happened to the bull?" Elias asked. Grandpa had a tendency to ramble.

"He left that bull tied to the post, and when we finished working the cattle, he and your mom went to their house and I went to mine. I thought about the bull tied to the post but I didn't say anything because I knew John hadn't forgotten. After supper I went to check just in case he had. I got about halfway to the pen when I saw your dad inside talking to the bull. I cursed myself for not bringing the shotgun. If he let that bull loose, I was afraid the bull would hurt him because he couldn't move very fast with his hurt leg. I picked up a stick and hurried, but I was too late. Your dad was already untying the bull. John said something to him and the bull threw up his head and snorted. I got a little closer in case John needed my help. I guess that bull figured he'd met his match. He walked over to the water trough and drank his fill and then meandered out of the corral to find his herd." Grandpa shook his head. "Your dad had a way with animals. That bull never gave him a moment's trouble after that. He knew who was boss. When Falcon dehorned the steer today, it kind of reminded me of your dad."

Silence filled the barn and Falcon was glad his mom had gone to the house. After all these years, the memory still hurt and each of them was feeling a tug on their heartstrings about the man who taught them everything they knew about being a cowboy, about ranching and about life.

"Let's all go get a beer at Rowdy's." Paxton was the first one to break the silence. "We're all home so let's celebrate the end of roundup."

"Sorry, Pax." Egan waved a hand as he headed for the door. "I have a wife waiting for me and that's better than a cold beer any day of the week."

"Come on, Egan. It's just one night."

Egan looked back as he weighed his options and Falcon knew thoughts of their father filled his head. "I'll call Rachel."

"Count me out," Jericho said. "I'll take care of the cow dogs and then I'm crashing for the rest of the evening."

"If Egan goes, you need to go, too," Paxton told him.

Jericho shook his head. "My drinking days are over. Spent half my life in bars, clubs and beer joints and it only brought me trouble. I'm content right here, but you boys have a good time. Call if you need me to drive you home." Jericho ambled out the door.

"Count me out, too," Jude said. "I have to help Zane with his homework."

"Help?" Elias laughed. "Zane is smarter than all of us put together. How can you help him?"

"I make sure he does it. He gets bored and I have to make him do it."

Phoenix threw an arm across Jude's shoulders. "What's it gonna hurt if you don't push him for one night? It's certainly not gonna hurt his grades and it'll help you to get out. When was the last time you went out to get a beer, Jude?"

"When you're raising a boy, there's more important things to consider."

"That's an excuse and tonight excuses don't work. We're going out as brothers. And that includes you, Falcon."

His younger brother was always full of it. But it was time to move on, to start living again and maybe, just maybe, start seeing other women for a change and not wait for Leah to come back. She'd come back and she'd made her choice. It was time for him to make his.

"They have a new waitress," Elias spoke up. "Her name is Brianna and she's a redhead and hot. Paxton and I have hit on her a number of times. Let's just let her choose from the Rebel boys. We're all available now. Well, except Egan. I'm ready to boot-scoot-boogie and raise hell. Let's go. No excuses."

Egan slid his phone into his pocket. "Rachel has a meeting at school that will probably last until about eight. I'm good for a beer."

Paxton slapped his leg. "Now we're talking. Bob makes good hamburgers so we'll eat there. All we have to do is shower and go. Who's with me?"

"I'm not," Grandpa said. "I'm going to my house and having a long nap. I'm like Jericho. My beer joint days are over."

"I'll fix you something for supper," Quincy offered.

Grandpa gave him a dark stare. "Now, boy, you go and have a good time. I got leftover pizza Cupcake brought me that will suit me just fine."

"Just don't put it in the microwave for five minutes like you did last time."

"Ah, I'll eat it cold or Cupcake will come over and help me."

Falcon knew that his daughter would. She'd do anything her grandpa asked. She had a soft heart, something she'd gotten from her mother. And how he wished he could stop thinking about Leah. Tonight he was going to do his best to forget her.

Less than an hour later the Rebels pulled into Rowdy's parking lot in three pickup trucks. Falcon, Quincy and Jude rode in Falcon's truck. Paxton, Elias and Phoenix came in another truck and Egan also came in his because he wanted to leave early. But they were there together to celebrate.

In boots and Stetsons they walked in and a hush came over the crowd. A group of men were around a pool table in the far left corner of the room. Several cowpokes were nursing beers at the bar and couples danced to an old Waylon Jennings song on the worn hardwood floor. The back of the bar was decorated with various neon beer signs and on the right wall were signed posters of country music singers who had stopped by while passing through. It was a small-town country bar with all the flavor of bygone days.

They gathered at a round table large enough for all of them. The wooden table and chairs were probably as old as Falcon and just as durable. People continued to shoot them narrowed-eyed glances. It wasn't often the town saw all the brothers together unless there was a family crisis, like when Egan got arrested a few months ago.

"Just for the record, there will be no fighting or getting drunk tonight." Falcon pulled out a wooden chair and sat down, as did the others.

"Come on, big brother, don't take the fun out of the evening." Phoenix plopped a bowl of peanuts on the table. "You go to a beer joint to have fun. Or have you forgotten?" Phoenix smiled slyly. "How old are you now?"

"Someone has to keep a clear head."

"Come on, Falcon," Elias said. "Leah has moved on and it's time for you to do the same. Things are looking up 'cause here comes the waitress—hot Brianna."

Falcon looked up to see a woman with red hair and green eyes—a beautiful woman. Her hair was pulled back to emphasize her pretty face. A half apron covered her jeans and her breasts pushed against a tight T-shirt. Yep, Elias was right. It was time to move on.

"What will you gentlemen have?" she asked politely and pointed a pencil at Elias and then Paxton. "And keep the sexist remarks to yourself."

Elias held a hand over his heart. "Oh, you've wounded me."

"Yeah, right."

"Don't pay him any attention," Paxton said. "These are our brothers and we're out to have a good time tonight."

She pointed the pencil around the table. "All of you are brothers?"

"Yes, ma'am."

"My, your poor mother."

Laughter echoed and Brianna smiled. Falcon didn't react. There was no zing. As he'd told his daughter, a person knew when something or someone was right for them. Brianna wasn't even in his sights because a dark-haired green-eyed woman was all he could see.

"What will y'all have tonight?"

She took their beer and hamburger orders and disappeared behind the bar. An old Willie Nelson song, "Mammas Don't Let Your Babies Grow Up to Be Cowboys," played on the jukebox and a few couples shuffled around the sawdust dance floor. The evening went well and everyone was on his best behavior. Or at least Elias, Phoenix and Paxton tried. Phoenix pinched Brianna's butt and she slapped him. That was the only altercation of the evening, until the McCrays walked in.

Gunnar was followed by his three brothers: Malachi and the twins, Ashton and Axel. Ruger, Ezra's son, and Homer, Isadore's son. This wasn't good. Gunnar was known to always make trouble.

Gunnar walked up to the table, followed by the others. He stopped next to Falcon. "You know, Rebel, I haven't seen Leah in town lately. Let's see, it's been about eighteen years now, hasn't it?"

"My wife is none of your business."

"She should have married me instead of a loser like you. How long did it last? Not even a year. I would've treated her like a queen. She probably knows that by now."

Falcon clenched and unclenched his fists, wanting to smash them right into Gunnar's face, but he remained still with superhuman strength. He took a sip from his beer, letting the cool taste calm his nerves.

"If I remember correctly, your wife, Cindy, left because you used her as a punching bag, so don't tell me how to treat a woman. That's the last thing you know anything about." He took another gulp of beer.

"Don't you know, Rebel, that drinking will kill you."

The reference to his dad took more restraint than Falcon had. Before he knew it, he'd stood up, his chair flying backward, crashing into the next table. The jukebox stopped playing and people scurried for the door. Without thinking, his fist connected with Gunnar's jaw and

Gunnar fell backward, his body sliding on the hardwood floor right into the jukebox. He jarred it so hard "Unwound" by George Strait blasted from the box.

But Falcon didn't have time to listen to the music. Malachi and the twins jumped him and knocked him to the floor. His brothers immediately joined the fight and all hell broke loose as tables splintered, glass shattered and bodies wrangled together in anger.

The blast of a shotgun brought everything to a standstill. Wyatt Carson, the sheriff, stood near the bar with a shotgun in his hand.

"Everybody on their feet," he shouted. "If any of you think of making a crazy move, this shotgun's gonna be aimed right at you."

Falcon's head felt as if it'd been pounded against the floor, which it had. His muscles ached and his fists were bruised, but he managed to get to his feet, as did the Rebels and McCrays, each family on different sides of the room, glaring at each other.

Wyatt walked a little closer, the shotgun pointed toward the ceiling. Stuart, his deputy, was behind him.

"You know I really hate having my supper interrupted and I'm not in the mood to do a lot of paperwork tonight, so here's what we're going to do, boys." He motioned to the bar with the shotgun where Bob was standing. "Put your cash on the bar, no change. If you have enough money to cover all the damages, I'm gonna be nice and let y'all go home because I don't have a big enough jail to hold a bunch of idiots."

Falcon felt like an idiot. He'd chastised his brothers for years for drinking and fighting and here he was right in the middle of it, the head of the family, the leader, the one they looked up to. It was strange to explain what 'was going on inside him. Adrenaline pumped through his veins and his pulse raced. He was living. Maybe not the right way, but he was alive and he was never more aware of that than he was at that moment. For years he'd been going through the motions, but tonight was different. He'd stepped out of his comfort zone and he wasn't all that upset with himself.

He laid cash on the bar like everyone else, maintaining his distance from the McCrays.

"Is there enough money to cover the damages?" Wyatt asked Bob.

"Well, Sheriff, you shot a hole in my ceiling. That will cost a little more."

"Stop complaining and count the money."

Bob nodded with a fistful of cash. "Yeah, that should do it."

Wyatt laid the shotgun over his shoulder. "You know I spend most of my time dealing with the Rebels and the McCrays. It's a good thing I'm a patient man. There's no need to give you a lecture because I know you won't listen. You never have." He glanced at Falcon. "I'm surprised at you. I usually can count on you to keep the peace."

Wyatt and Falcon had gone to school together and they knew each other quite well. Wyatt was right, though. Falcon had spent years trying to keep his brothers under control. He wasn't going to apologize for losing it tonight.

He reached for his mangled hat on the floor, trying not to wince. "Sometimes, Wyatt, a man just has to fight."

"He started it," Malachi said. "He hit Gunnar, and there's no way we'd let him get away with that."

Wyatt turned his attention to Malachi. "According to what Bob told me on the phone, Gunnar started it with his big mouth."

Malachi looked away.

He pointed toward the door with the shotgun. "Go home, clean up your bruises and don't come back into town until you cool off."

"Why do we have to go first?" Axel asked.

"Because I told you to, or you can spend a few nights in jail. Your choice."

The McCrays found their hats and filed out the door, casting angry glances their way.

"What a pitiful sight you guys are." Wyatt shook his head, taking in the bloody noses, black eyes, scrapes and bruises. "Go home, and please stay there for a while. Give me a rest for about a month."

His brothers ambled toward the door and Falcon stopped by Bob. "If that doesn't cover everything, just give me a call."

"Thanks, Falcon. I wanted to hit Gunnar myself."

Falcon tried to smile, but his face hurt too much. As he passed Wyatt, he said, "You're a little wild with that shotgun."

"You guys don't usually come into town at the same time. It's enough to make my heart stop."

"Yeah, right." Falcon followed his brothers out the door. They stood outside in the moonlight, looking at each other.

"Damn, can you believe it? Falcon lost it." Phoenix slapped his leg in amusement. "He hit Gunnar so hard the man's head will never be the same. He turned on the jukebox."

They all laughed, standing as brothers against a common foe. Egan rubbed his bruised jaw. "Now I have to go home and explain this to Rachel."

"She'll kiss it and make it better," Elias chortled in a weird voice. "Lucky dog."

"Let's go home and nurse our wounds," Falcon said.

"I bet ol' Gunnar won't be able to open his big mouth tomorrow." Phoenix threw an arm over Elias's shoulder, either in camaraderie or for the support. Falcon couldn't tell which. "Falcon came unwound, didn't he? Bam. He put Gunnar in another time zone."

Their voices trailed away and Falcon made his way to his truck, followed by Quincy and Jude. Yep, he'd lost it. It was a night of bonding with his brothers that Falcon wouldn't forget anytime soon. He was definitely moving on. He got a lot of anger and resentment out of his system, mainly on Gunnar.

But it wasn't enough to shake her image from his mind.

Chapter Nine

A time for reality...

Moving on came with a headache—a big one. Falcon crawled out of bed with moans and grunts. He wasn't sixteen anymore, but last night he was wild, reckless and crazy. Responsibility was supposed to have curbed all that. As he'd told Wyatt, sometimes even a levelheaded man could be pushed to the edge.

He managed to shower, shave and get dressed. There was a knot the size of an egg on the back of his head where Malachi had tried to beat his brains out against the hardwood floor. Falcon had finally got a fist in his face and Quincy and Jude pulled Ashton and Axel off him. Hitting heads with the McCrays was a waste of energy. Why hadn't he learned that by now? Maybe because the fight had just been about letting off some steam.

In the hallway, he banged on Eden's door and winced. That wasn't smart. It made his head pound more. "Time to get up."

"I'm already up, Dad," Eden called.

Now he had to face his mom and he wasn't looking forward to that. She was pulling biscuits out of the oven and gaped at him, taking in his bruised face. "What happened?"

He poured a cup of coffee, not even considering lying to his mother. "We had a little altercation with the McCrays last night."

"What?"

"Gunnar was goading me and I reacted. I usually let his slimeball words wash over me. But last night I'd had enough."

She set the biscuits on the stove, her eyes worried, and Falcon felt a kick to his heart. "I've always told you to use your judgment, so he must've said something hurtful and vile."

"Yeah, and I'd just as soon forget it." He sat at the table, hoping the discussion was over.

"Did all my boys get in the fight?"

"Yes, ma'am, we tore up Rowdy's last night and the sheriff was called. Luckily, no one was arrested, but we had to pay for the damages."

"Was anyone hurt?"

"No, just some bruises."

She wiped her hands on her apron. "You haven't been the same since Leah was here. I'll never understand how she can hurt you and Eden like she has."

He took a sip of his coffee, not wanting to talk about Leah. "She's out of our lives for good now. At least we don't have to wonder anymore."

"That's what makes me so…"

Eden bounced in, preventing his mom from going off on Leah. "Dad, I'll be late today. I have school stuff." She grabbed a piece of bacon off a platter on the stove and turned, her mouth falling open at the sight of his face.

"Dad?"

He shifted uneasily, since he preached good behavior to his daughter all her life. "It's nothing."

"But you're hurt. Did you get in a fight?"

Jude walked in and poured a cup of coffee, and his mom and Eden gaped at his black eye.

"Did you fight with Uncle Jude?" His daughter glared at him.

"No, I didn't fight with Jude."

Zane ran into the kitchen. "Eden, did you see...? Oh..." His voice trailed off as he noticed Falcon.

Falcon scooted back in his chair. "Okay, listen, Jude and I and the other brothers got into a fight with the McCrays last night. It's over and I don't want to hear any more questions."

"Did you kick a—"

"Eden."

"I was just gonna say, well, yes, I hoped you kicked butt."

Falcon got up and placed his cup in the sink. "I'm going to work."

As usual, his daughter couldn't let it go. "Bryce McCray is always saying snide things to me and if he does it again, I'm going to smack him."

He pointed a finger at her. "You only smack if he touches you inappropriately. Do not react to silly words. He just wants you to react."

"But—"

"No *buts*."

"Dad!"

"If you hit for no reason, you will not barrel race. You will not do a lot of things."

"You need to do what I did," Zane told Eden. "Dudley McCray is always calling me a nerdy geek and I told him if he didn't stop, I was going to tell my daddy and he would tie his big fat neck into a knot and my other uncles would make a pretzel out of him. He hasn't bothered me since."

Jude frowned at his son. "You never said Dudley was bothering you."

"I handled it, Dad." Zane stuffed bacon and eggs onto a biscuit. "I didn't hit him or anything. I used my mind instead because Dudley has only one oar in the water, if you know what I mean."

"I don't like you keeping secrets from me."

Zane shrugged. "Okay, Dad."

"I'm not taking anything off Bryce anymore, either." Eden wasn't letting it go but his head hurt too much to get angry.

"You're not fighting a boy, that's all I'm going to say. If I hear anything to the contrary, you're going to have one upset dad on your hands. You got it?"

His daughter glared at him and he walked out of the room, followed by Jude.

"I don't want to go through that again," Jude said. "I don't want my kid to think fighting is good. I don't want him to think I approve of it."

"Yeah, it's hell when you're trying to teach your kids things, and then you turn around and do exactly what you're trying to tell them not to do. I guess you never get too old to screw up."

"Yeah."

"The legacy lives on," Falcon murmured. "The Rebels and McCrays will be fighting until the end of time."

"Mmm."

Nothing else was said as they walked to the barn. As

they neared the entrance, Jude said, "I'm sorry about Leah. I know that was hard on you."

"Last night was about moving on. Now I'm wondering just how many bad decisions a man can make in a lifetime."

"You did all the right things, Fal. Don't beat yourself up. Women are just hard to understand."

"Really?" He slapped his brother on the back. "We picked doozies, didn't we? Love wasn't enough. That's just about all the introspection I'm doing today. Eden is all that matters to me and I'll make sure she's happy no matter what I have to do."

"But you'll never forget Leah."

Falcon knew his brother spoke from experience. Jude would never forget Paige. The Rebels had no problem finding women. It was holding on to them that was the difficult part. Yep, he would never forget Leah. He would check the mail once again today to see if the divorce papers had arrived. Then it would be over and he had to face reality. His life did not include Leah anymore.

"I CAN DRIVE YOU," Anne Thornwall said from Leah's bed, eating Truman Chocolates.

"You're supposed to be taking it easy. The baby's due in six weeks."

Anne made a face. "I feel like a cow. I was never this big with the girls."

Leah sat at her dressing table, combing her hair. "Alma's been driving me to my appointments. It's not that far to the medical center and she's a very good driver." She laid her brush down. "I don't know what's wrong with me. I feel so sick. Dr. Morris is afraid I might have a virus or the flu. He's run more tests and I have to go in and get the results. The surgery is in three days and nothing can go wrong now."

Anne pushed up from the bed, which was an effort for her. Anne was blonde and blue-eyed just like her daughters. She was not only beautiful on the outside she also had an inner beauty that encompassed everyone around her.

"It's probably just nerves. You've been very jittery lately, which is understandable. So much is at stake with this operation, but I'm optimistic that everything is going to work out. They'll remove the tumor and you'll get a chance to go back and be with your family."

Leah gripped her hands together. She wanted to be optimistic, too, but life hadn't been too kind to her, so she couldn't get her hopes up. In a way she felt this was her punishment for doing what she'd done to Eden and Falcon.

"I want that more than anything, but too much has happened and I can't live with daydreams."

"Just be positive."

Anne rubbed her stomach. She did that a lot. "This baby is a real kicker. The girls didn't kick like this."

Leah touched Anne's swollen stomach. "I'm trying not to think unhappy thoughts, but I may never be able to see this precious angel."

Anne's face crumbled. "Don't say things like that." She gave Leah a hug. "To cheer you up I'll tell you a secret if you promise not to tell."

Leah turned in her chair to face Anne, a light in her eyes. "You know, don't you?"

"Yes," Anne whispered in case David was near and she didn't want him to hear. "I know we promised we'd wait until the birth, but I couldn't stand it."

"Does David know?"

"Heavens, no." Anne waved her hand. "We decided to wait and he's waiting. He wants a boy so bad and I just had to find out."

Leah tilted her head and stared at her friend. "From the look on your face I'm guessing it's a boy."

Anne smiled. "Yes. I'm so happy. Of course, David says he'll be just as happy if it's another girl, but I know that man sometimes better than I know myself and he wants a boy. This time he's going to get one."

Leah stood and hugged her friend. "I'm happy for both of you. The baby couldn't have better parents."

"Oh, please. Look how we screwed up with Callie."

Leah reached for her purse. "Callie's fine. She was just testing you." Callie got in with a bad crowd and ran away from home because she said her parents were smothering her. But it had all worked out and Callie was in college now and doing very well.

Feeling sick, Leah sat back down with a hand to her forehead. "I don't know why I'm so ill. Maybe I am coming down with something. I just want to crawl in the bed and not get out, but my stomach feels like I'm fixing to throw up."

"I better go with you."

"No, you won't. You go home and rest. Alma and I will be fine. I'll call you later."

"I'll just be home worrying."

Leah got to her feet again. "I'll call you the minute I know anything."

"You better."

Leah hugged Anne again. "I'm happy about the baby."

"Don't you dare tell David."

"My lips are sealed."

THIRTY MINUTES LATER Leah sat in Dr. Morris's waiting room with Alma. "I hate that you have to sit here."

Alma shrugged. "What else have I got to do? I would do anything to make sure you're healthy for this surgery. I brought my knitting and I might look through a few of these magazines for some new recipes."

"I wish Miss Hattie was here."

Alma patted Leah's hands she had clasped in her lap. "She would be beside herself, but we all knew that tumor had to come out sooner or later. And now is the time. You'll be fine. I've been praying and praying and I believe in prayer. So don't you worry. This matter is in someone else's hands. Someone stronger than you and me."

"I'm so blessed to have you in my life."

"Humph. I put up with Miss Hattie more years than I want to remember. I lost track of the number of times I quit or the number of times she fired me. She was one stubborn lady, but I loved her. And she wanted me to take care of you and I will fulfill her dying wish. Not because she asked me, but because you're such a sweet lady. I would do anything for you."

"You're gonna make me cry."

Alma patted Leah's hands again. "Hush, now."

"Ms. Rebel," the nurse called, and Leah got up and followed her down the hall to Dr. Morris's office. Leah was surprised to be shown into the office. Usually it was an examining room.

"Is there a reason Dr. Morris is seeing me in here?"

"He just wants to talk to you."

"Thanks." Leah sat in a brown leather chair facing a large oak desk. Medical books covered one wall. The room was spotless—much like the doctor, who was meticulous and orderly.

She'd sat in this office the day he'd told her about the tumor. It had been discovered after the accident, but the doctors didn't tell her until she was back on her feet and looking forward to returning to Horseshoe and facing Falcon and Eden. The news had hit her hard and her dreams had come crashing down again.

The news had also upset Miss Hattie and she urged Leah not to have the surgery because of all the uncertainties. She knew Miss Hattie was thinking of Leah's best interests, but Leah should've had the surgery then when the tumor was benign and small. Now the risks were so much greater.

It seemed as if every decision she made was the wrong one for her and her loved ones. She opened the locket she wore around her neck. Inside was a photo of Falcon and Eden. She was hungry for pictures and news of her daughter. Leah had found Eden on Facebook. With Callie's help, she was able to friend her daughter without her knowing who she was and she saw pictures that made it easier to get through each day.

The door opened and Dr. Hyde Morris came in carrying her medical file. They shook hands and he took his seat at the desk. Of medium height and balding, Dr. Morris was dressed in his usual dark slacks and white doctor's coat.

"You're looking well," he said.

"I don't feel well."

He scooted his chair forward and opened her file on the desk. "That's what I want to talk about."

"Did you get the test results?"

"Yes."

She expected him to say more, but he was silent and that bothered her. He usually was a talker.

"And…"

He flipped through her file. "Tell me how you're feeling?"

"Lousy. My head hurts and I'm sick to my stomach most days. Does that have anything to do with the tumor?"

"Partly. But we're getting close to the surgery now and I want to check every angle. How's your vision?"

"It comes and goes. Some days it's bad, as I've told you."

"Recently you visited your husband and daughter?"

The question threw her, but she answered, "Yes, I wanted to see them before the surgery."

"We've talked about a lot of things, but you never said how the visit went."

She moved nervously, crossing her legs, having no idea where this was leading. She felt it was none of his business.

"It was very sad and upsetting, but uplifting in a way. I got to hold my daughter and though she was angry at first I felt she came around in the end."

"And the husband?"

"He was very angry, but like our daughter he came around, too."

He leaned back in his chair. "You're still adamant about them not being here for the surgery?"

"Yes. They don't need to be burdened with me now. We said our goodbyes and they've forgiven me. That's all I wanted to hear."

"Leah…"

"Have you been talking to David?"

"We're colleagues and I talk to him just about every day. And yes, I've talked to him about you because we want you to recover and have a full life ahead of you."

"But you've said there could be debilitating side effects."

He leaned forward. "I had to be honest with you. The tumor is rare, benign and slow growing, and usually goes undetected until it causes problems. In your case we discovered it from the MRIs of the head injuries you suffered during the accident. At that time your other health issues took precedence, but we've closely monitored it. As I've showed you on the MRIs, it's positioned in the ridge along the back of the eyes and it's going to be very difficult to remove without damage to your vision. After all this time, it's now showing abnormal cells and that's the reason we need to get it out before it becomes malignant. You are already experiencing some of its effects with your vision and there could be changes in your hearing, your thinking and your motor skills. I'm just giving you all the facts, but I'm a damn good neurosurgeon and I plan to give you the best chance at a life."

Leah frowned. "But you're not certain that you can?

"No. With surgery there are always risks."

"You've already told me all this. Is there a reason you're going over it again today this close to the surgery?"

He removed a piece of paper from the file and came around the desk and leaned against it facing her. "This is going to be a very difficult surgery and recovery. My goal is to have the patient as relaxed as possible, and also optimistic."

"I'm praying with everything in me that you can remove it without any damage to my vision."

"Usually a patient wants family around at this time."

She sighed. "Dr. Morris, what are you getting at?"

"How do you feel about your husband?"

"That's really none of your business." The words came out before she could stop them.

He nodded. "It probably isn't, but due to the results of this test, I've canceled the surgery."

Leah's pulse raced. "Why? Do I have a virus or the flu?"

"I wish it was that simple. We could just postpone if it was that."

"What is it, then?"

He looked at the paper in his hand and then at her. "You're pregnant."

Chapter Ten

A time to decide...

"What!"

"You're feeling sick because you're pregnant."

Her body trembled and she wrapped her arms around her waist, her hand inching down to cover her stomach. *Pregnant.* Again. With Falcon's child. An overwhelming sense of joy washed over her and she stopped trembling. She should be angry, upset, but all she felt was a joy of the precious gift she'd been given.

"This presents many complications." The doctor's voice penetrated her fog.

"What?"

He held up two fingers. "I now have two patients and I have to figure out what's best for both of you. I've canceled the surgery until I can consult with an obstetrician, an anesthesiologist and a neonatal doctor."

"This is hard to believe," she said, trying to take it in, but her mind wasn't working. All she could think was that she was pregnant.

"What happens now?"

"I've operated on women before who have been pregnant, but the tumor was discovered while they were pregnant. Your situation is slightly different. I'll postpone the surgery until I can speak with doctors who have dealt with this type of high-risk pregnancy before. After the consultation, we'll talk again. The tumor has to come out. We should've done it a year ago or even before that, but at that point it wasn't life threatening."

"Will the tumor harm the baby?"

Dr. Morris walked around to his desk and sat down. "No, not the tumor itself. I'm more concerned with the drugs you'll be given and the effect on the fetus. Starting today you'll only take acetaminophen for the headaches."

"Okay." She glanced down at the clasped hands in her lap. This was the last thing she'd expected when she walked into his office today. So many questions ran through her head and so many emotions threatened to choke her. When it was just her life, the decision was easy. Now there was a baby and she would do nothing to harm it. This was her second chance and she was going to grasp it with everything in her, even if it meant risking her life.

She looked at the doctor. "If I have the surgery now, will the baby be at risk?"

"The drugs you'll be given will be a concern and there's a possibility you might abort it."

"I want to carry this baby as long as I can. Since the tumor is not harming it, I will do just that."

"I advise talking to the doctors first. "

She shook her head. "It won't change my mind. I want to give the baby every chance."

"Leah…"

"I'm serious about this." She put her hand over her stomach.

"It's your decision."

"Yes, it is." Her bravado wavered a little. "Not that it will make a difference, but how will waiting affect my health?"

"The tumor will continue to grow and possibly become malignant and then your chances of survival are considerably lower. If we get it out now, your chances are better. Losing your eyesight is a main concern, hearing, too, but I suggest a neurological evaluation every two weeks to stay on top of it. And if you agree, I'll contact the obstetrician and set up an appointment."

"Yes, I'd like that."

He closed her file on the desk. "As you pointed out, it's none of my business, but I strongly advise you to call your husband. It's his child, too."

She didn't even ask how he knew the baby was Falcon's. It was a good guess because she wasn't dating anyone. David and Anne had tried to set her up many times. But she was never interested. She was a married woman and even though she had left her husband she would never break her vows.

"That's my decision, too."

"Do you mind if I talk to David about this?"

She stood on shaky legs. "Yes, I mind. I will tell them tonight and then you can talk to him all you want, but I'll be the one to tell them."

He inclined his head. "Call me if you have any problems. My secretary will set up your next appointment."

Slipping the strap of her purse over her shoulder, she said, "Sometimes things happen for a reason and I know there's a reason somewhere in all this. I don't understand it, but I will accept it and carry this child as long as I can."

"Talk to David and Anne."

"I will." She gripped her purse strap tighter.

"And please talk to your husband."

Walking out of the room, she felt stronger than she'd ever had before in her life. This baby was a gift and she would treat it as such. No matter what happened in the days, weeks and months ahead she would accept her fate with grace and dignity and give this child a chance at a life. She'd bailed on Eden, but she would never harm this baby.

She was silent on the way home and Alma didn't say much, either. When they walked into the kitchen, Leah said, "I need to tell you something."

Alma grabbed her chest. "Oh, Miss Leah, don't tell me bad news."

"I'm pregnant."

Alma frowned. "What?"

"I'm going to have a baby."

"But…who? What about the tumor?"

"My husband. I've decided not to have the surgery just yet to give the baby a better chance."

"Oh, Miss Leah." Alma clutched her chest again. "What about your health?"

Leah looked down at her stomach. "It doesn't matter. Only the baby matters."

Alma hugged her. "God has a plan, Miss Leah. Just you wait and see. Everything will work out. You have to trust and believe. I come from a strong line of Catholics and we've been believing for years and I will continue to pray for you and this little one." She placed a hand on Leah's stomach. "Have you told the Thornwalls?"

"I'll do that tonight."

She called Anne and invited them over, saying she

had something to tell them. The Thornwall family arrived and they sat in Miss Hattie's stylish living room, including Callie and Calise because Leah had invited them also. She was close to the girls and she wanted them to know.

When she told them about her visit with Dr. Morris, they stared at her like a tree full of owls—big eyes and their mouths forming big Os.

David was the first to react. "Excuse me. What did you say?"

She told them again about the pregnancy and her decision to wait before the surgery.

David got to his feet, shaking his head. "How did this happen, Leah?"

Callie laughed. "Dad, you should've figured that out by now."

David glared at his daughter. "This isn't funny. Leah has a tumor that needs to come out."

"I have gone over everything with Dr. Morris. The baby will have a better chance if I wait. This is my second chance to be a mother and I want that more than anything."

"Have you told your husband?" David asked.

Leah knew this was coming and she braced herself. She had conflicting emotions about calling Falcon and she still hadn't decided. He had a right to know, she kept thinking, but she still worried that he might force her to do something she didn't want. She needed time to get her thoughts straight.

"Not yet," she replied.

"Leah, he needs to know now."

On and on it went until Leah grew weary. Anne stayed out of it as her husband continued to apply pressure.

Finally Callie interrupted. "Okay, Dad. We've heard your opinion and that's all it is—your opinion. It's Leah's body and she has a right to make her own decisions and I stand firmly behind her."

David turned on his daughter. "You know nothing about this."

Callie threw back her blond hair. "Really? Because I'm just a teenager? I don't need to be an adult to respect someone's wishes. I love Leah and I'm not forcing my opinions on her and you shouldn't, either."

Anne stood with the help of Callie and put a hand on David's arm. "Honey, let's go and give Leah some peace. We can talk about this again tomorrow."

Seventeen-year-old Calise, better known as Lissie, hugged Leah around the waist. "I support you in whatever you want to do."

Leah hugged her back. "Thank you, sweetie. That means a lot to me."

David studied her for a moment and then came over and folded her in his arms. At that moment she wished they were someone else's arms. She pushed the thought away immediately.

"My mother always taught me to be respectful, so I'm going to accept your decision, even though I know it's wrong, but as the women in my life have pointed out I need to respect your wishes."

"Thank you. I appreciate that."

He drew back. "But risking your ire, I'll say again your husband needs to know and he needs to be here."

Leah was tired of the bickering and she didn't want to start all over again. "I have a lot of thinking to do."

"Good," David said, and the family walked out the back door. Silence settled in the house like an old friend.

It was what she needed now. Peace and quiet to make all the right decisions for herself, her baby and, yes, for Falcon.

Lying in bed that night, she reached for the locket around her neck and held it in her hand as if she could feel Falcon's presence. If she called him, he would come because that's how he was—honorable and loyal. But she didn't want him to come out of a sense of duty. She wanted him to come out of love.

She had to wonder if that was even a possibility after all they'd been through.

FALCON WAS FEELING better than he had in a long time. Eden had her first rodeo and she did very well. She came in third and was mad because her time could've been better, she'd said. So she was now practicing every chance she got. He never realized how determined she was and how much she liked barrel racing. He would support her every way he could, but she was still going to college. Which made *him* stubborn, as Eden had pointed out several times. He was sticking to his guns, though.

It bothered him that his daughter had only mentioned her mother a couple of times. He expected a lot of questions, but Eden was busy with school and barrel racing and seemed to accept Leah's decision to leave them behind for a new life. The divorce papers still hadn't come and he wondered about that. But he didn't call. He left well enough alone. He had enough problems running the ranch without adding more to his plate.

The family was having a meeting in the office. They were going into the winter months and they wouldn't be as busy as they had been in the spring and summer. But they had cattle and horses that needed feeding regularly in the cold months.

His mother sat beside him at the desk and the others lounged around the office.

"Paxton and Phoenix are going to be rodeoing through December and Egan wants some time off to finish his house. He and Rachel want to be in by Christmas. Does anyone else want time off? This would be the time to do it." Kate looked around the office at her sons.

"I'll be helping Egan," Jericho replied. "But I'll also be here to help with the feeding."

"Thanks, Rico, but take some days. You've earned it."

"Thank you, Miss Kate, but I'm happy right here."

"I'm going to a paint auction, and it's going to take about a week at the end of October. And I might take some extra days," Quincy said.

"Fine." Their mom nodded.

"Anybody else?" Falcon asked. "Jude, Elias and me can handle just about anything that comes up here."

"Who said I was going to be here?" Elias piped up.

"You have to speak up, son," his mother told him. "We can't read your mind."

"Thank God for that." Elias laughed.

"So you want some time off?" Falcon looked at his brother.

"Damn straight."

"When?"

"The boy doesn't know what he wants." Grandpa, sitting in the only comfortable chair in the room, added his opinion. "He's gonna take me to Abilene in about two weeks."

"May I ask why?" Falcon really didn't want to know

the answer. He had no idea what Grandpa was up to and most of the time it was best not to know.

"There's a woman up there I want to see. Went to high school with her and we've been writing each other."

"For heaven sakes, Abe. Aren't you tired of chasing women?" His mother was in full attack mode now and the meeting was getting out of control.

"It's none of your business, Kate, so stay out of it."

"When you use my boys as your personal servants, it's my business." His mother stiffened beside him and Falcon thought he should put a stop to it, but sometimes it was best to get all the anger out in the open so he let them go at it.

"They're John's sons and my grandsons!" Grandpa shouted.

"Why don't you say what's really bothering you, Abe?"

"I don't know what you're talking about."

"You blame me for John's death." His mother said something that brought all of them to full attention.

Grandpa pointed a finger at her. "You should've stopped him from drinking so much."

"Don't you think I tried? I poured whiskey down the drain more times than I can count, but he always went back into town and bought more. How was I supposed to stop that? And why didn't you? You were his father. He looked up to you. Why didn't you stop him?"

A tear rolled from Grandpa's eyes and everyone was frozen in place, not knowing what to do. They'd never seen Grandpa cry before and it was a heartbreaking moment.

"I tried. Don't you think I tried?" Grandpa's words were barely audible but they heard them.

Egan knelt by Grandpa's chair and patted his arm. "It was nobody's fault, Grandpa. I always felt if I'd spent more time with him he wouldn't have drunk so much. I think we all felt that. But no one's to blame for what happened but Dad. There was nothing any one of us could have done differently, especially Mom. Dad wouldn't let anyone fight his battles, you know that."

"Yeah." Grandpa brushed away a tear. "He was pigheaded. I guess he got that from me."

Jude rubbed Grandpa's shoulder. "Yep. We all have our share of that."

Silence enveloped the room as each dealt with their thoughts of their dad.

Elias was the first to speak. "Grandpa, this is the first I've heard of a woman in Abilene. Not that I'm against chasing women, but I thought we were going to look at quarter horses."

"What?" Falcon glanced up. "Quarter horses? We have all the horses we need here."

Grandpa glared at Elias. "You had to open your big mouth."

Elias shrugged.

"Why are you interested in quarter horses?" Falcon asked again.

Grandpa looked him square in the eye with a obstinate expression Falcon knew well. "Cupcake's birthday is coming up in January and I want to buy her a good horse so she can work cattle."

"Cupcake has all the horses she needs. Quincy just gave her a very expensive paint and she has a quarter horse, Starfire."

"Starfire has no fire," Grandpa shot back. "She needs a better horse."

Falcon scooted forward in his chair. "Let's get something straight. My daughter is not going to be working cattle. There are enough of us to do that. She's going to start having a life of her own away from Rebel Ranch."

"Why?" Grandpa demanded. "Why are you so anxious to get rid of her? She belongs here with us."

And a new topic was born that tore at Falcon's insides. "Do you think it's easy for me to make these decisions for her? I'd love for her to stay here, but I want more for her. I want her to experience a world away from here and if she wants to come back, then it's her decision. It's not easy letting go, Grandpa, but I have to and I hope you understand that."

"I'll miss her," Grandpa murmured.

"We all will," Quincy added. "But Cupcake is not going far and we'll all be there to support her barrel racing. She's getting very good."

"I'm buying her a new truck, something that can pull a horse trailer better than that little Ford she has," Falcon said.

"What am I going to give her, then?" Grandpa asked.

"I thought you were going to give her the silver dollars your grandfather gave you," Falcon said.

Grandpa slapped his leg. "Damn, I forgot I promised her those. Now I have to find them. Not sure where I put 'em."

"I'll help you look," Quincy promised.

Their mother joined the conversation again. "I'm giving her a big party that day, which happens to fall on a Saturday. It'll be a family affair and I'll invite some of her friends. Is that okay?"

"Yes, Mom. She'd be disappointed if we didn't celebrate her birthday."

"Paxton and me are taking her out drinking for her birthday," Phoenix chimed in.

Falcon frowned. "You're not taking my daughter out drinking."

"What you don't know, big brother, won't hurt you."

"But I'll hurt you if I find out about it."

Phoenix two-stepped across the room. "You have to catch me first."

"Idiot," Falcon mumbled under his breath, and everyone laughed, bringing some much-needed relief to the tension in the room.

Soon they all filed out to go to work, including his mom, and Falcon welcomed the quiet. What a meeting. It was emotionally draining to put up with the bickering between his mother and grandpa, but this morning got a lot of resentment out of their systems. He hoped. But with the Rebels that was all he could hope.

The landline rang and he picked it up. "Rebel Ranch."

"I'd like to speak to Falcon Rebel, please."

It was a man's voice Falcon had never heard before. "This is Falcon."

"I'm David Thornwall."

Leah's new love. Falcon was stunned and said the first thing that came into his mind. "Why are you calling me?"

"If you care anything about your wife, you will come to Houston to see her. That's all I'm going to say."

"What are you talking about?" Visiting Leah and David was the last thing he wanted to do.

"I can't say any more than I have. Her address is…" He rattled off an address and Falcon jotted it down because there was a pad in front of him. "I'm breaking her confidence, Mr. Rebel, and I don't do this lightly."

"I don't understand this. Leah told me she was starting a new life and—"

"I said what I had to. The rest is up to you." The line went dead.

Falcon sat in a stupor. What the—? He got up and paced around the office. None of this made sense. He had Leah's number and he pulled out his cell to call and then put it back in his pocket. There was only one way to get to the truth, but he didn't have time to go to Houston.

He had a lot going on at the ranch today that needed his attention. Traveling to Houston would take the whole day, but it sounded serious. He reached for his hat and went out the door.

The family had just talked about vacation days. Falcon decided to take one to find out what was going on with Leah.

Chapter Eleven

A time to talk...

Falcon found the address without a problem. The Bellaire subdivision was off Loop 610 and easy to find. He drove down tree-lined two-story homes with manicured yards. When he found the number, he pulled up to the curb. It was a brown two-story brick and the crepe myrtles were still in bloom. The garage door was down, but a BMW was parked outside. It wasn't Leah's car.

He had no idea what he was going to find there. The answer was inside, so Falcon got out and walked up to the front door. He rang the bell and waited. A tall man in a dark blue suit opened the door.

"Mr. Rebel?"

Falcon nodded. "Where's Leah?" He wasn't in the mood to exchange pleasantries.

"Please come in." The man stepped back and still Falcon hesitated.

"I'd rather not. Why did you call me?"

"If you'll come in, I'll explain. Leah's upstairs."

Falcon didn't have a choice if he wanted answers. He removed his Stetson and stepped inside a large foyer with an Oriental rug. The house was formal, just the opposite of Rebel Ranch, where everything was casual. He had the urge to wipe his boots. Instead, he followed the man into a large living area and then into a kitchen. A Mexican woman came from another room, carrying a laundry basket. She glanced at him and then at David.

"You're interfering, Mr. David. She's not going to like it," the woman said, shaking her head.

"Take care of the laundry, Alma."

The woman made a face and disappeared back into the room.

"Have a seat, Mr. Rebel," David said.

"Just tell me what's wrong with Leah."

"I'll get coffee." David walked over to a big Keurig coffeemaker. Coffee was the last thing Falcon needed, but he could see David wasn't listening to him.

David placed two filled coffee cups on the table. Falcon looked at them and asked, "What's wrong with Leah?"

"Please sit. This is going to take a while."

Falcon gave in to the inevitable and pulled out a chair. Before he could sit, a very pregnant blonde came into the room.

"David, who was at…" The blonde's words trailed off as she noticed Falcon. She frowned at David. "What have you done?"

Falcon could almost see the sweat popping out on David's forehead. "Mr. Rebel, this is my wife, Anne."

Wife? What was going on? He was totally lost for words. The man had a wife!

"Nice to meet you, Mr. Rebel, but if you'll excuse me, I'm going home." She reached for her purse on the granite countertop and glanced at her husband. "When you get home, expect a lot of attitude."

"Anne—"

The woman slammed the door.

David ran a hand through his hair. "I'm going to receive a lot of flack about calling you, so please sit down and let's get this over with. I feel I'm doing the right thing, but maybe I shouldn't have called."

Falcon hooked his hat over the back of a chair and took a seat. "What's going on here?"

David sat across from him. "I'm just going to say it, Mr. Rebel. Leah has a brain tumor."

The color drained from Falcon's face and his stomach roiled. "W-what?"

"Leah had severe head injuries from the accident. It was at that time the doctors discovered the tumor. It was very small, benign and not life threatening. She had so many other problems the doctors decided to wait before addressing the tumor. It took years before Leah could get back on her feet and the doctors continued to monitor the tumor. She probably had it for a very long time, maybe even as a child."

Falcon swallowed hard. "Was that the reason she never came home?"

"Yes. As soon as she was better, her plan was to return to her family. She didn't want to call you while she was down because she didn't want you to have to take care of her."

"I'm her husband. I should've been called." Anger began to uncurl in his stomach.

"That was her decision."

Falcon tried to stay focused. "After all this time, why hasn't the tumor been removed?"

"She was set to do it about four years ago, then my mother had a stroke and Leah put it off because she said she couldn't do it while my mother was sick. That's the type of person Leah is. She was at my mother's bedside every day and my mother got better. Once again she rescheduled the surgery to remove the tumor." David shrugged. "Leah wanted to go home so badly but there always seemed to be something to stop her."

"What stopped her this time?"

"My mother had another stroke and was bedridden. We hired nurses around the clock, but Leah wouldn't leave her. Leah's childhood was really sad and…"

"She told you about her childhood?" Once again anger started to take hold. Why would Leah tell him and not Falcon?

"She told my mother first and my mother told me. Somehow my mother and Leah made a connection. They were like mother and daughter. As much as Leah wanted to go home, she couldn't leave my mother. Mom died a few months ago and Leah made plans to remove the tumor. But by then the tumor had started to grow and now has abnormal cells. It's pressing on her optic nerve and some days she can barely see. She's dizzy quite often and has headaches."

"She fainted at our house."

David frowned. "She didn't mention that."

"I put it down to nerves, but I can see now it was much more."

David nodded. "Yes."

Falcon's thoughts were all jumbled but he kept coming back to the same old question. "Why didn't she want me here when she had the surgery?"

"As a doctor, and as someone who's talked to the neurosurgeon many times, we feel the tumor is now interfering with her thinking. She gets very angry when we mention that. Her main concern was that she didn't want you to have to take care of her if after the surgery she was blind or incapacitated. She didn't want you or her daughter to witness that."

"But we're her family."

"The family she ran out on, as she puts it. She blames herself and just cannot put you or her daughter through that."

"Has the surgery been scheduled?"

"Yes, it was supposed to have been Monday, but it was canceled."

"Why?"

"Another complication has come up."

Falcon looked at the man and knew something bad had happened. He braced himself. "What? Has it gotten worse?"

"I've told you all I can tell you, but I feel as her husband you need to be here. She will have to tell you the rest of it."

"Listen, you called me, and I want to hear all of the story. I want to hear the whole damn truth of why you kept my wife here in Houston when she could have come home years ago."

David held up his hands. "It's always been Leah's decision. We have never held her here against her will. Honestly, I felt she was afraid. She was afraid you would never forgive her and she was afraid her daughter might hate her. She kept putting it off and…"

"What?"

"Anne, what happened to…" Leah stood in the doorway. She glanced from David to Falcon. Her mouth fell open and she quickly recovered from the shock of seeing him. Her gaze centered on David. "I'll never forgive you for this." She turned on her heel and left the room.

Falcon slowly got to his feet. "Evidently she doesn't want to see me."

David also stood. "There's never been anything but friendship between Leah and me. She's been a very good friend to my family and my mother. We were blessed to have her in our lives, but I feel I have risked our friendship now. I believe in my heart your wife needs you, though." He headed toward the back door. "I'm going home to face my wife's wrath. Take the stairs and Leah's room is the first door on the right. Good luck, Mr. Rebel. I hope Leah comes around."

"Thank you for calling. I'm not real sure how to handle this, but I know I'm not leaving until Leah tells me the whole truth."

"Give her a chance to be angry. Hang in there because I believe she still loves you. She may never admit that though. Now, I have to walk home because my wife has taken the car."

"Do you need a ride?"

"No, thanks. I live about three blocks away and I need the walk to clear my head to face Anne."

The man walked out, and Falcon stood there wondering what he should do next. It wasn't hard to figure out. He picked up his hat and found his way to the living room and the stairs. He had no idea what the rest of the story was and he had to hear it out to the very end. When he'd started this trip, he never expected anything like this. Leah hadn't come home because she was sick. She didn't want him to take care of her. How could she think that? She was his wife and it was his duty to care for her. How had their lives gotten so messed up?

LEAH PACED IN her room. She was so angry at David she wanted to scream. How dare he interfere in her life! She took a couple of deep breaths and sat down. She had to get control of herself because she knew she had to face Falcon. He was here and he wasn't leaving. Of that she was sure.

She tensed when she heard the tap at the door.

"Leah, may I come in?"

She curled her hands into fists. What was she going to say? If she told him about the baby, he would take over. She had to be devious and lie to send him away. Her stomach cramped at the thought.

"Go away, Falcon, I don't want to talk to you."

The door opened and he came in. Tall, strong and all male. It would be a test of her strength to stand against him.

"I'm here, Leah, and I'm not leaving until we talk." He walked over to the bed and sat down, facing her. He placed his hat on the bed. She'd seen him do that a million times. That hat went with him more places than she ever had.

"Why didn't you tell me about the tumor?"

Her mouth went dry. "It…was my choice. I did what I thought was right for me, you and Eden."

He threw up his hands. "How can you say it was right when it kept you from coming home year after year? I should've been the first person called when you recovered your memory. I'll never understand why I wasn't. You have a tumor. So what? We're married and we can work through this. That's the way *right* looks to me."

"It wasn't your choice. You're not the one with the tumor. You're not the one who left."

"Still…"

She jumped up and walked over to the window. This wasn't going to be easy—his way was always right.

She turned to face him. "I made a lot of bad choices, but they were my choices to make. Please understand that."

"I don't. If you had come home years ago you would've been able to see your daughter grow up."

A pain pierced her heart. "Don't you think I wanted to? Every day I ached to hold my baby."

"Then why did the tumor stop you? According to David, it was benign and not life threatening."

She stared down at the area rug on the hardwood floor. How did she explain her feelings to him? No one was going to understand how she felt at the time.

"Leah…"

"Because I was afraid. Okay? Returning to face you scared me to death. I knew you would never forgive me and I was so afraid Eden would hate me. It was years before they completed all the surgeries and then I had to learn to walk again. It was a long road to recovery and by then I knew you had moved on and my daughter, well, facing y'all paralyzed me with fear." A tear trickled from her eyes and she brushed it away. "Looking back, I guess I took every excuse to postpone the time when I would have to account for what I'd done."

Falcon stood. "We deserved to know that you were okay. Did you ever think about that?"

"But would it have made my leaving any easier to bear? And if I had called, you would've insisted on coming here and taking over, the way you usually do."

"That's what you feared most? Me 'taking over your life,' as you put it?"

"Did you ever see me as a person? Someone with

thoughts and ideas and emotions that might differ from yours?"

He frowned. "What kind of question is that? Of course I saw you as a vibrant woman with needs and desires and dreams I wanted to be a part of. A part of you."

She brushed away another tear, hating that he was so kind and she was struggling just to say the right words to keep him from finding out about the baby. She wondered why she wanted to keep the baby from him. He didn't deserve that. Just as he hadn't deserved her leaving him years ago.

"Leah..." He took a step toward her.

"No, please don't touch me. I can't think when you touch me."

"Why don't we stop trying to place blame about the past? It's over. We can't go back and change a thing. Let's move forward now and talk about the tumor. Why did you cancel the surgery?"

She sucked air into her lungs. "I didn't. The surgeon did."

"Why?"

"It's a long story. As I've told David and the doctors, this is my decision, and I choose to wait for a while before having the surgery." Her breath stalled and she prayed for courage. "There's really no need for you to be here and I absolutely do not want you to tell Eden. It would only upset her."

"I don't keep secrets from Eden. I've been honest with her, even when it hurts. And if you're worried about your daughter hating you, well, when she finds out you don't want her here when you're going through a traumatic ordeal, she really will hate you. You don't know her very well. She's a nurturing person. I don't know where she got that from, but she helps take care of Grandpa and she's the light in his eyes. She makes sure he has food to eat or anything else he wants. She would fuss over you like a mother hen. I can't promise not to tell her because I respect her more than that."

The room swayed and Leah put a hand to her head. So many things were crowding in on her and for the first time she realized she wasn't thinking straight. David was right. She had to concentrate. She had to make the right decision.

"Are you okay?"

"Just a little dizzy." She sat down in a chair before she fainted again. She had to be careful about that because she didn't want to harm the baby. Thoughts rumbled around in her head and she couldn't make sense of any of them, but she knew she had to start being honest. She had to stop hiding behind the past. She'd made mistakes and she had to correct them now.

"The thought of surgery is frightening," she said in a low voice. "I've had so many—my head, my face, my chest and both legs. Every time I think about the surgery I get cold chills and I back out. That's the simple truth. I used Miss Hattie to put it off. I'm a coward. I'm afraid I'll lose my sight or, worse, be in a vegetative state. I'm so scared."

Falcon didn't say anything and she looked up to see his face a strange shade of white. Finally, he said, "I'm here, Leah, and I will be here with you to face it. Whatever happens I will be here with you. We're family. You don't have to put the surgery off any longer."

She glanced at her hands that were numb clasped in her lap. "Yes, I do."

"Why? You don't have to be afraid. David was right in calling me. We can get through this. You're not alone."

"It's more than that and I'd rather you let me go through this alone. I need to do this alone."

He frowned again. "Leah, I'm not trying to control you. I just want to help you. I want you to get better so you can enjoy your daughter."

She tried to stand, but her legs were shaky. She had to tell him, but she feared she would then have no choices left to her. In that moment, she knew she had to trust him. Falcon was somehow different from the young boy she'd married. He was a man now and she had to be adult enough to tell him about their baby.

"I…I asked to have more time before the surgery. I need that time."

"Why?"

She looked at him then and saw all the worry and concern in his beautiful eyes and it made it easier to say the words. "Because I'm pregnant."

Chapter Twelve

A time to give in...

"Pregnant! You mean..." Falcon was glad the bed was behind him because his legs grew weak and he plopped onto it. It took him a moment to recover.

"It happened that morning in the hotel. And as it is with us we forgot to use protection. It happened that way with Eden. Being older and more responsible doesn't seem to matter when it comes to—"

"That's why David called me." Falcon's brain began to function again. He slowly got to his feet. "And you weren't going to tell me, were you?"

Leah put a hand to her head and Falcon knew she was avoiding the question.

"Were you?" he shouted.

"Okay!" she shouted back. "I'm just trying to figure out all of this and I wasn't sure what to do."

"Not sure? It's my kid. Why would you keep this from me?"

"Because..." Tears rolled from her eyes and Falcon fought to remain steadfast. He wasn't going to weaken. She wasn't going to get away with keeping something like this from him.

"This is my second chance to be a mother and I want that with all my heart. I'm just afraid you'll want me to have the surgery earlier than I want."

"Oh, man." A flicker of remorse tugged at his conscience. "The tumor. For a moment I forgot about it." He took a deep breath and calmed himself. Getting angry wasn't going to help anyone. "What did the doctors say?"

She brushed back her hair on the right side of her face. She never did that on the left, where part of her hair was missing. He thought of all that she'd been through—and now he'd caused her more pain. He had to stop being angry and think about this rationally. He was known for that, wasn't he?

"Dr. Morris wants to consult with an obstetrician and an anesthesiologist before making a decision."

"He might suggest surgery while you're pregnant?"

"Yes, he says he's operated on women who've had tumors removed while pregnant."

"Will the surgery harm the baby?"

"Dr. Morris said they've had amazing results and the babies have all been born healthy, but there are risks. I want to wait so the baby is stronger and I'll be less likely to abort it."

He sat back on the bed, needing a moment to gather his thoughts. He'd never expected this, and he was feeling blindsided and vulnerable and wondering what was the right thing to do for Leah and the baby. In his mind, though, there weren't any easy answers.

Leah's head was bent, her dark hair falling forward. She was pregnant with his child and once again it was his fault. In that hotel room, he had been so angry with her and that all changed when he'd touched her. It had always been that way between them. He just couldn't understand why she couldn't trust him. Why she couldn't turn to him?

"Am I such a monster?"

Her head jerked up. "What?"

"You didn't call me after the accident and you weren't going to tell me about the baby. Why would you do that? Do you intentionally try to hurt me?"

She shook her head. "No. It really isn't that. When it comes to you, I'm weak and I give in to whatever you want. This time, I have to be strong for this baby because I want to carry it. I want to be a mother again and I don't want anyone to take that from me. Even you. And for the record, I would have eventually told you. I was just trying to come to grips with what I have to face now."

"I'm not going to strong-arm you. I want us to do this together. Could we talk to the doctor?"

She fiddled with her hands in her lap. "Sure, I'll call him."

He stood and reached for her hand in her lap. "You and I are facing this together. Understand?"

"Really?"

"I just want to know details."

Leah brightened instantly. "I don't know this Falcon. The one who was screaming a minute ago I know."

"When you're raising a little girl you learn patience and sensitivity. She has taught me more than anyone in my life, even my dad. She's brought out the softer side of me." Falcon didn't even know he felt that way until he said the words. His daughter had changed his whole world and if he did nothing else on this earth, he wanted to be a good father.

"I'd love to get to know her, too."

"Well, then, let's talk to this doctor and see what the future holds."

Thirty minutes later they sat in the doctor's office waiting to talk to him. Leah was nervous. She kept fiddling with her hands and Falcon didn't know how to make the situation easy for her. He didn't know how to make it easier for himself, either.

When they were called back, Falcon braced himself for the biggest decision of his life. The doctor went over everything in detail and even used diagrams and computer images to show Falcon where the tumor was and how he would remove it. When Dr. Morris mentioned cutting into Leah's skull to remove a portion so he could reach the tumor, Falcon grew anxious. Could Leah survive that? Would she be okay? Questions beat at him, but he stayed focused on what the doctor was saying.

"I would like to get the tumor out now," Dr. Morris said. "I've consulted with a qualified high-risk obstetrician, Dr. Judith McNeil, and her advice was, as long as Leah's life is not at risk, to wait as long as possible to give the fetus more time. But the final decision is yours."

Falcon met Leah's gaze. "What do you want to do?"

"I want to wait," she replied in a low voice.

"Dr. McNeil wants to see you to evaluate the fetus."

The answer to the problem was easy, but by the paleness of Leah's face he knew it wasn't.

Falcon had so many questions. "Can she carry this baby to term? And what are the risks to her health? To the baby?"

"When I feel there is a risk to Leah's health, I will strongly advise to remove the tumor. The biggest risk is the tumor becoming malignant in that length of time.

And, of course, her eyesight is at risk. You would have to discuss the baby's prognosis with Dr. McNeil."

"You will closely monitor Leah?"

Dr. Morris looked at Leah. "Yes. I want to see Leah every other week. My concern is once your hormones kick in it will cause the tumor to grow. I want to be notified of any changes like coughing up blood, anything out of the ordinary." The doctor flipped through Leah's file and pulled out a business card. He pushed it across the desk. "This is a card from Dr. McNeil. I've worked with her before and she's the best in her field. My secretary has made an appointment and it's on the back."

Leah reached for the card. "Thank you."

Dr. Morris picked up some papers and handed them to Falcon. "Here are some articles and literature on tumors in pregnancy. They should answer any lingering questions you have."

"Thanks."

"We'll take this one day at a time." The doctor stood and shook Falcon's hand. "It's nice to meet you and I'm really glad you're here for Leah."

The ride back to the house was in silence until Leah said, "Thank you for being here. I know it's my fault you weren't, but I never realized how much I needed you."

"As I told you before we'll get through this together. You don't have to do this alone, Leah. I don't know why you feel you have to, but we won't go into that. We're not arguing anymore. It can't be good for you or the baby."

"May I ask you a question?"

"Sure."

"When David called you, what did he say?"

Falcon negotiated the heavy traffic. "He said if I cared

anything about my wife, I'd come to Houston, and he gave me the address."

"Did you think that was odd?"

"Yes. I didn't have a clue what he was talking about since you said you were going to marry the man. I hadn't gotten the divorce papers, so I decided to come and see what was going on for myself."

"So you came out of a sense of curiosity?"

"I guess." He had a feeling she wanted him to say something more, but for the life of him he didn't know what it was.

He drove up to the house and they got out and went in. The aroma in the kitchen was mouthwatering. The Mexican lady had been cooking, and Falcon realized how hungry he was.

"Come, sit down," the woman said. "It's time for lunch and I fixed a big meal for Mr. Cowboy."

Falcon removed his hat. "You didn't have to do that."

"Miss Leah has to eat healthy and I make sure she eats that way every day."

"Falcon, this is Alma, my friend and housekeeper," Leah introduced them. "And Alma, this is my husband, Falcon—or Mr. Cowboy, if that's what you want to call him."

"Whatever." Alma pointed to a door. "There's a bathroom if you need to wash up."

Falcon hooked his hat on the back of the chair and headed for the bathroom. When he came out, only Alma was in the kitchen.

"Miss Leah's washing up. Sit," Alma instructed in her brusque manner.

Once again he obeyed and thought his brothers would

get a good laugh out of that. "I don't mean to be nosy, but do you live here?"

"Yes, sir. I do. I have my own set of rooms and I'm here for Miss Leah whenever she needs me."

"Good, because I have to go back to the ranch for a while and I don't want Leah to be alone."

"So you're planning on coming back?" Alma placed dishes on the table.

"Of course."

Alma thumbed over her shoulder. "Have you told her that?"

"No, but I will."

Alma shook her head. "She can be stubborn, but I guess I don't have to tell you that."

"Who's stubborn?" Leah asked, coming back into the room and taking a seat across from Falcon.

"The food smells delicious," Falcon said, to change the subject. "What is it?"

"Smothered steak with mushroom gravy, mashed potatoes, green beans, salad and banana pudding. It should stick to your ribs."

Leah placed a napkin in her lap. "Alma's a great cook."

"Yeah, yeah." Alma nodded her head. "I already ate so I'm going to my room to call my sister and leave you two alone."

"You don't have to do that," Falcon told her. But the woman wasn't listening as she disappeared through a door.

They ate in silence for a moment and then Leah said, "I never cooked for you."

"What?"

She picked at her food. "Your mother did all the cooking and I never had a chance to cook us a meal."

Falcon never realized that, or that she had actually wanted to. How could he have missed it? "My mom would have been glad to have the help."

Leah looked at him with a dark stare. "I did the dishes, Falcon, and cleaned up. That's different than cooking a meal for you and me. Alone."

He laid his fork down. "I'm sorry I wasn't more aware of your feelings at that time."

She shrugged. "I don't know why I brought it up."

"Because it still bothers you."

She stirred the mashed potatoes with her fork. "I guess it does. We were going to clean out your parents' old house and move in there, but we never did."

"No." He leaned back in his chair. "Quincy, Egan and Elias finally cleaned it out and got rid of some stuff and stored the rest in a barn. They live there now. Well, Quincy and Elias do. Egan got married and moved to his own place."

"Who did he marry?"

"Rachel Hollister."

"Judge Hollister's daughter?"

"Yes, and they're very happy."

"That's nice."

There was silence again, and he knew she was thinking about all the mistakes they'd made. For once he was seeing them up close and personal, and most of them were his fault.

"I have to go back to the ranch for a while to tell Eden."

She placed her napkin on the table. "I know."

"She's going to want to come here to see you."

"I can handle it now. I want to see my daughter, but there's no need for you to stay here. You have to run the ranch and I know you have a lot of responsibilities on your shoulders. I'll be fine and I'll take very good care of the baby."

"Look at me, Leah." She met his eyes and he recognized the terror hidden in the green depths. He was feeling a little of that himself. "This is my child and I will be here as often as I can. I have six brothers and if they can't run that ranch, then we're in trouble. I just have to go home to prepare Eden and my family, but I'll be back. I will not let you go through this alone."

"Okay," she replied in a forlorn voice.

He reached for his hat and got to his feet. "I'll come back as soon as I can."

"There's no rush, I'm fine."

He watched her for a moment and recognized that expression. Alma was right. His wife was stubborn. But he now knew why. She didn't want him to watch her suffer, so he didn't read too much into it.

He twisted the hat in his hand. "I was thinking that Eden and I might spend some time with you. She has school, but I think I can work out something so she can do homework on the computer. "

Her chin jutted out as she got to her feet. "That would be nice, but sometimes I can't see and I get real sick. I don't want my daughter to witness that."

"Wait until you get to know your daughter and you'll change your mind. Just let us be here, that's all I'm asking."

She walked him to the door and for a moment nothing was said. "I don't know what to say," she finally mumbled. "I hurt you so much and I'm struggling to figure out if I'm making the right choices and decisions."

"Just relax and let us, your family, help you."

She nodded and he put his hat on his head and walked out the door. He didn't attempt to hug her or touch her in any way because he knew she didn't want that. Not now.

Driving away he couldn't help but think that he shouldn't be leaving. She needed him, but they also had a daughter who had to hear the truth. Falcon had to find the right words to break it to Eden gently. He wasn't looking forward to it.

LEAH WATCHED THE truck from the window until it turned the corner and was out of sight. Wrapping her arms around her waist, a calm came over her, something she hadn't felt in a long time. The future was so dim, but now with Falcon by her side a glimmer of hope began to burn in her heart. She wanted to live and she wanted to have this baby. She wanted it all and she would fight to have it. But she knew it could come with a big price.

Feeling dizzy, she went upstairs to lie down. She'd been so angry with David and now she could see how mistaken she'd been. She was making wrong decisions and everyone knew that. Later, she'd call David and apologize.

She pulled the locket from her blouse and stared at it. The two people inside were all she ever thought about. Somewhere inside her heart she had to forgive herself and move on. All she had to do was stop feeling the guilt and the pain of leaving them.

Curling up on the bed, she thought about the question she'd asked Falcon. About why he'd come to Houston. She was hoping he would say because he still loved her. But he hadn't. As her eyes grew heavy she wondered if he could ever love her again, the way he had when they were teenagers. That was her fairy tale. Her dream, and she prayed she lived to see it come true.

If only…

WHEN FALCON DROVE into the yard at Rebel Ranch, his brothers had two trailers backed into the supply barn and were unloading salt and mineral blocks and bags of feeding cubes for the winter. He got out of his truck and walked to the entrance. Elias, Paxton and Phoenix were horsing around as usual.

On Elias's back was a sign that said Punch Me. As if Elias needed a reason to fight. That had to be the handiwork of Phoenix, the joker of the family.

Grandpa walked by Elias and punched him in the back.

"Hey, Grandpa, what'd you do that for?"

"Don't wear a sign if you don't want to get punched."

"What?" Elias turned round and round trying to see his back, and Phoenix bent over laughing, as did the other brothers. "I'm gonna kill you, Phoenix." Elias made a dive for his younger brother, but it was hard to fight someone who was laughing so hard.

"Stop it," Falcon shouted. "I'm not in the mood for this childishness."

Phoenix rolled to his feet, tapped his heels and saluted. "Yes, sir."

"Cut it out, Phoenix. I need to talk to the family."

Silence fell in the barn and the brothers gathered around. His mother came in at that moment and asked, "What's going on?"

"I have some bad news and I want to get it over with because I have to talk to Eden when she comes home from school."

"What is it, son?" his mother asked.

"It's about Leah." He told them the whole story and watched their faces turn to stunned disbelief. "I'm taking some time off so I can be with her. I'm also going to talk to Eden's teachers to see if she can do her classes online because I feel that Leah would want her close."

"Of course, son. You do what you have to. Don't you worry about the ranch. You need to take care of your family."

"Rachel can probably help with getting Eden's classes set up online," Egan said. "I know she'd do anything to help."

"Thanks, I'd appreciate that. I have to tell Eden, and I don't know how she's going to take this."

"We're here for you." Quincy stepped forward.

"I know, and I'll need each of you to pick up the slack around here and try to stop fighting and keep this ranch on an even keel."

"You can count on us," Elias said.

Paxton laughed.

"What?"

"Just do it," Falcon stated. "And stop baiting each other. Life is too short."

That brought on the silence again and no one knew what to say. Falcon didn't, either. He requested that they give him time to talk to Eden before anyone came to the house. They agreed.

An hour later he sat in the den with Eden by his side, once again searching for words. He told her the truth because that was all he had.

She stared at him with big rounded eyes and an expression on her face he couldn't describe.

He gathered her in his arms like he had when she was

three years old and a truck had run over her dog. "She's hurting, baby, and she needs us. I'm going to talk to your teachers to see if you can spend some time with her. I think she would like that."

Eden straightened. "Would she? I mean, she wasn't even gonna tell you about the baby. That makes me mad."

Eden's attitude scraped across his last good nerve.

"I mean, she was here, like, two hours and you had sex, and she still left like she did before. Moonbeams don't mean too much to her."

He didn't want to talk about this with his daughter. He got to his feet. "Your mother needs us now."

"What about the times we needed her?"

He didn't know where Eden's anger was coming from, or maybe he did. She was remembering that little girl who grew up without a mother—a mother who could have come home but didn't.

"I'm not going to force you to go if you don't want to. It's your choice. But I'll be leaving soon to make sure your mother and the baby are okay. Yes, she made some bad choices, and I hope somewhere in that big heart of yours you will find a way to forgive her. Because, baby, if you don't, you might regret it later."

Eden hung her head. "Is she gonna die?"

Now Falcon knew where all the anger was coming from. Eden was afraid of losing her mother for good.

"The doctor didn't say that, but there could be complications from the tumor, like losing her eyesight, or it could become malignant, and then her chances of survival are lower."

"No, Daddy." A tear slipped down her cheek.

Once again he took her in his arms and held her. "I know you're having conflicting thoughts."

"I'm just mad at her for not telling us the truth." She wiped her face on his shirt.

"What do you want to do, baby girl?"

She scrubbed at her eyes with her fists and then glanced at him with a stubborn expression just like Leah's. "I'm going."

"I'll call Rachel to see if she can get things started with your schoolwork and you go pack."

Within the hour they were packed and ready to leave. Falcon decided he didn't want to be away from Leah in case she needed him. Like his daughter he had conflicting thoughts, too. And a little anger. And he, too, would have to find forgiveness in his heart. He really hoped that was possible. But no way was he walking away from his child. That might make him controlling, but then that part of him was hard to change.

Chapter Thirteen

A time for family...

After showering, Leah slipped into some pj's she'd bought at Victoria's Secret while out shopping with Anne. The bottoms were soft silky pink capris and the top was a white tank top trimmed in lacy pink. It came with a skimpy robe and Leah had loved it on sight. It wasn't something she usually wore at night, but this evening she was feeling better than she had in a long time.

Earlier, she had talked to David and Anne and apologized for her behavior. David was kind, as always, and she had to admit that her thinking was off and she was happy he had called Falcon when she had been unable to.

It was hard to explain all the emotions churning in her. Looking back, she tried to figure out why it was so important to her to stay away from Horseshoe. Guilt was one thing. But for her, the past weighed her down until she couldn't think straight. It had a lot to do with the tumor affecting her thinking. She should've listened to the doctors and not been so adamant about her decisions. She could see that now.

Sitting on the bed, she reached for lotion and applied it to her arms and legs, wondering when Falcon and Eden would come back. After all the years she had stayed away from them, she couldn't believe how anxious she was to see them now. It was like Falcon had said. They were family.

"Miss Leah," Alma called.

"I'm in here," Leah responded.

Alma walked in with a glass of milk. "Thought you might like this before going to bed."

"Thank you. That was so sweet." She took the glass and placed it on the nightstand.

"I bought a gallon so there's plenty to make this baby as strong as possible."

"You're spoiling me."

"Mmm. Do you need anything else?"

"No, thanks." A smile tugged at Leah's lips. "My daughter is coming, Alma. You'll get to meet her."

"I'm looking forward to it, and if she's anything like her mother, I'll love her."

Leah was silent for a moment and thought how she knew nothing about the daughter she'd given birth to. But she wouldn't let that bring her down. She was taking steps forward and she would concentrate on that.

"Good night," Alma said, walking out of the room.

"Night."

Leah picked up the glass and took some sips. She wasn't that crazy about milk, but she would drink anything to make this baby healthy. She finished the milk and took the glass into the bathroom to rinse it out. Her cell rang and she hurried into the bedroom to find it. Her purse was on her desk and she grabbed it and found her phone. It was Falcon. Her heart raced.

"How are you?" he asked and she soaked up the soft tone in his voice that she didn't hear often enough.

"I'm fine and the baby is, too."

"Would you like some company?"

"You mean tomorrow?"

"No. I mean now. I'm about two blocks away."

"Is Eden with you?"

"Yes."

Her heart raced even faster and she took a deep breath to calm herself. "I'll open the front door."

"We'll be there in a minute."

She placed the phone on the desk and slipped into her robe. Hurrying downstairs, she had to make herself stop. She didn't want to fall. As she opened the door, the cool night air rushed in. The yard was well lit, so it was easy to see the big truck as it pulled up to the curb.

Falcon got out, tall and imposing, but Leah's attention was on the person coming around the front of the truck: her daughter. She paused by her father, and Leah wrapped her arms around her waist as she waited.

Eden said something to Falcon, and he frowned—even she could see that from the front door. Falcon strolled toward Leah and Eden trailed behind, which was not a good sign.

They stood there, staring at each other, words eluding them. Falcon broke the silence.

"Let's go inside, ladies."

Leah stepped back. "Come in. Come in." They walked into the living room and Falcon and Eden sat on the sofa. Leah took a wingback chair facing them.

Years ago Leah had very little self-confidence and even though she'd gained some of that over the years she was still struggling to be the woman she should be. She didn't know if she'd ever make the full transformation into a confident, independent person. But she was determined to give it her best, even with Eden glaring at her.

"Why didn't you tell us about the tumor?" Eden asked with a bite in her voice. "Why did you have to lie?"

Leah knew she would have to answer some hard questions and this was one of them. She didn't evade it or put it off. She was honest. "I didn't want to be a burden to your father after what I'd done. I wanted to be completely well before I came home."

"Did you ever think I might need my mother, sick or not?" The words were fired with the force of a bullet and Leah felt the piercing pain.

Tears threatened, but Leah fought them off. Her daughter had every right to be angry and Leah had to dredge up her courage to tell her side of the story. She told her about the day she'd left Rebel Ranch. She didn't leave anything out, even sharing her awful childhood and her feelings about her own mother, and Leah's fear of hurting Eden. Then she told her about the accident, the long road to recovery and her fear of removing the tumor.

"I'm sorry you had to go through all that," Eden mumbled. "I just don't know why you didn't come home when you were better."

"Fear," Leah admitted. "It's a powerful thing when you've hurt someone like I hurt your father and you. Falcon is a very strong and forceful man and I felt he would just never forgive what I'd done and…and I felt you were better off without a mother like me. A mother who would leave her baby didn't deserve second chances. That was my attitude, and I couldn't get past that. I—"

"I'm hungry," Falcon said, interrupting her and getting to his feet. "We haven't had supper and I know there's some banana pudding left from lunch."

"Oh, yes, I can make you a sandwich or something." Leah was glad for the reprieve and followed Falcon toward the kitchen.

Falcon stopped to look at his daughter. "Eden?"

"I'm not hungry," she muttered and hung her head, her dark hair falling forward, covering her face.

Leah wanted to say something to ease her pain, but words were useless now. Eden had to come to terms with what happened because Leah couldn't change it. They all had to accept it and move on.

In the kitchen, Leah pulled out lettuce and tomatoes. "How about a bacon, lettuce and tomato sandwich?"

"Sounds great." Falcon sat in one of the bar stools at the granite island. "Eden is just angry and she doesn't stay angry for long, so give her time."

"I can take it," she replied, getting bacon out of the freezer. "I didn't really expect anything less. I buy cooked bacon. Is that okay?"

"Sure."

As she opened the package, she asked, "Are you angry, too?"

The question took him by surprise and his expression changed. "Yeah, I guess a little. Like Eden, I don't understand why you couldn't come home."

They were never going to understand how she felt at the time or how fragile her emotional state was. She placed strips of bacon on paper towels and then onto a paper plate. "Then I guess it's safe to say that you're never going to forgive me."

"I didn't say that, Leah. We all need some time to adjust to this new situation. I can't just snap my fingers and make us a family again. Too much has happened. But I will be here for you and the baby. You don't have to doubt that for a minute."

She didn't. Although she was happy he was here, her heart wanted so much more. But, like he'd said, too much had happened. The days ahead would be trying.

"I decided I'm hungry," Eden said from the doorway.

"Well, come on in, baby girl. Your mother is making bacon, lettuce and tomato sandwiches."

"I can help." She walked to stand by Leah and stared at the bacon on the paper plate. "What's that?"

"It's cooked bacon you buy at the grocery store," Leah told her.

"Grandma fries hers."

"I remember. Kate makes everything from scratch."

"Yeah," Eden replied. "What do you want me to do?"

"There's tea in the refrigerator. You can fix your father and yourself a glass."

Falcon took a seat at the table, watching them. He'd left his hat in the living room, and she liked it when he didn't wear his hat. Of course, she liked it when he wore his hat, too. There was just something vulnerable about him without a Stetson, though. So many years and she just wanted to keep staring at him. She brought herself out of her reverie and placed the bacon in the microwave.

Alma stomped in wearing her flowered chenille robe with cold cream on her face and a satin thing she always wore around her hair when she went to bed. "What's going on…? My, oh, my." Her eyes centered on Eden.

Her daughter stepped forward. "Hi, I'm Eden."

"You don't have to tell me that, child. You look just like your mother."

"That's what my dad says."

"It's true." Alma's eyes swung to Falcon. "You made a fast trip, Mr. Cowboy."

He thumbed toward Eden. "I had to bring the kid."

Alma clapped her hands. "This is so nice."

"It is, isn't it?" Leah continued to make the sandwiches and Alma noticed. "Let me do that. You go visit with Mr. Cowboy."

Leah shook her head. "No. I'm fixing supper for my family. I got it, but thanks."

Alma hesitated, but eventually went back to her room. Leah was determined to spend this time alone with Falcon and Eden.

"We can use paper plates instead of real plates," Eden said. "That way no one has to do dishes. Zane and I are the dishwashers at the ranch."

"You put dishes in the dishwasher," Falcon reminded her.

"It's still doing dishes."

"You poor thing."

Leah laughed, something she hadn't done in a long time. It vibrated through her whole body and made her feel alive again. This was what she'd been missing— the rest of her.

"Who is Zane?" she asked. He had to be the boy Leah had seen with Eden when she'd gone back to Horseshoe.

"Jude's son," Falcon replied.

"Is he the only cousin?"

"Yep." Eden carried glasses of tea to the table. "He's enough." Her daughter turned to her. "Paper plates?"

"Oh, yes." She'd gotten sidetracked hearing about the family. "We have some in the pantry. I'll get..." The room swayed and Leah grabbed the granite countertop. "Oh."

"Are you okay?" Eden shouted.

In an instant Falcon was at her side, holding her elbow. "Can you walk to the table?"

She nodded, still feeling dizzy, but she made it to the table with Falcon's help. A look of fear was on her daughter's face and Leah hated that. "I'm okay. I just have these every now and then. I'm okay, really."

"Can I get you anything?" Eden asked.

"A glass of water would be nice." She didn't really want water, but she felt Eden needed to do something to make herself feel better.

Falcon sat next to her. "How often do you have these spells?" His voice was low so Eden couldn't hear.

"I'm okay, Falcon."

Eden brought the water, preventing Falcon from saying anything else. Sipping, Leah had a moment to regroup. Falcon got up and went to help Eden with the meal. Nothing much was said as they ate and Leah felt a pang of regret that they were now being careful of what they said to her or what they did.

Afterward, Eden put the few dishes they'd used in the dishwasher and Falcon went to get their suitcases out of the truck. Leah and Eden went upstairs and she showed her daughter to her bedroom right across from hers. Falcon brought in the suitcases.

"What's in this thing, Eden? It's heavy."

"My stuff. That's all." She took the case from her father.

Falcon and Leah left Eden putting up her things. "You can use the room next door," Leah told Falcon.

His eyes narrowed. "Fine, but since you're having dizzy spells and you fainted at the ranch, I'd feel better being closer to you. Anything could happen. Like I said in the kitchen, we just can't be husband and wife again so fast. We need time, but you also need me."

"I'll be fine, Falcon."

"No, you won't, and no matter how much you protest I will never believe it. I'll put my things in the other room, but I'll sleep in yours."

She was stunned for a moment and then walked into her room so Eden wouldn't hear them. "I don't think that's a good idea."

"Why?"

"Because...you know..."

"You don't think we can sleep in a bed without having sex?"

Warmth suffused her whole body and she feared it showed on her face. "We haven't so far."

"I'm staying in here, Leah. That might make me controlling, but I'm not leaving you alone for something to happen during the night. I need to be here with you."

The warmth settled in her heart. "Okay." She gave in easily.

While Falcon went to put up his stuff in the other bathroom and to take a shower, Leah took a moment to gather her thoughts. Things were happening too fast but she was powerless to stop what she had started by returning to Horseshoe and her family.

She sat on the bed. Had she done the right thing in returning to Horseshoe? Of course, she told herself, she had no other options. For years she yearned to see her daughter and Falcon, and she had to take that step for her own sanity. She could handle a little attitude from her daughter because she never realized until today how much she needed her family.

Falcon was saying good-night to Eden and she could

see him through the doorway. He had on pajamas. When did he start wearing pajamas? When they'd been married, he wore briefs or nothing at all, but having a little girl in the house had really changed him.

Should she say good-night to Eden or just leave well enough alone? Not saying good-night wasn't an option. She walked into the room as Falcon was leaving. "Night, baby girl."

"Night, Daddy," Eden called.

Leah hesitated only for a moment. "Good night, Eden," she said.

"Night," Eden replied, snuggling under the comforter.

"If there's anything you need, I'm just across the hall."

"I won't need anything."

The words were clipped, and Leah gave up. "Good night, then."

She went back to her room and paused as she saw Falcon stretched out beneath the sheet and comforter. It had been a long time since they'd shared a bed and her nerves tingled in anticipation.

"You call her baby girl?"

Falcon punched up his pillow. "Yeah. I guess she's getting a little old for that."

Leah removed her robe and laid it over a chair. "I don't think she'll ever get too old for that. You have a good relationship with her."

"Are you wearing that to bed?"

She looked down at her pj's. "Yes. Where else would I wear it?"

"Um…nothing. It's just…"

Flipping off the light, she paused for a second and then slipped into bed.

Silence ensued as the darkness enveloped them. Suddenly, his voice came. "How come you don't want me to touch you?"

She turned on her side to face him. "I didn't say that."

"Yes, you did. Earlier today."

"I was feeling really conflicted then."

"And now?"

She took a long time before she answered because she wanted to get it right. "I'm glad you're here. I really am."

"You'll let me know if you're feeling dizzy or faint?"

She thought about his question for a moment. "Yes."

"We can get through this and hopefully both you and the baby will do well."

And then what? she wondered, but what she said was, "When did you get to be so understanding?"

"Life either makes you or breaks you and I decided after my dad's death that I had to be strong for Eden and my family. I couldn't yell or scream or take out my frustrations on them. I had to learn control."

"I'm so sorry about John. He was a really nice person, but even I could see he was tormented by the shooting of Ezra McCray."

"Yeah. It has affected us all."

"I'm sorry I wasn't there for you."

"Don't worry about it."

"Falcon."

"Hmm?"

"Do you know what happened to my aunt?"

"She sold the house in Horseshoe and moved closer to her older daughter in Fort Worth. Nancy eventually moved there, too. Your aunt died about five years ago."

"Oh." A pain settled around her heart at the loss of

someone who had loved her and tried to raise her right. "She must have been so disappointed in me."

"Not really. She just said she'd wished she'd been there for you."

Even though her aunt was strict, she had a loving heart, and Leah felt the loss in a way she couldn't describe.

There was silence again and all Leah's thoughts turned to the tumor and the baby and her uncertain future.

"Thank you."

"For what?"

"For being so understanding."

"Try telling that to my brothers."

She smiled in the darkness, remembering how the Rebel boys had fought. Being Rebels they didn't seem to have a choice but to use their fists. It was in their DNA, Kate Rebel had once said.

Without a word, she curled up in the bed, loving the scent of manly soap and a masculinity that was all Falcon. What would he say if she asked him to hold her? Three little words ached in her throat and she wanted to say them so badly, but it was too soon. She rested her head on the pillow and drifted into peaceful sleep, knowing he was only inches away.

Chapter Fourteen

A time to be strong...

Falcon settled into city life. He thought he would feel like a caged animal since he was used to the outdoors and spent very little time in the house. The tension between Leah and Eden kept him on his toes, though.

He'd only planned to stay a couple of weeks, but soon found Leah needed him. Awake at 5 a.m. every morning, he checked to make sure Leah was okay and then went to his room to dress and call Quincy and his mom. They went over ranch business so Falcon could keep up with what was happening. So far everything was fine.

Eden had classes in the morning and she couldn't come out of her room until all her assignments were done. That was the rule.

He and Leah spent a solid week in doctors' offices. They met with the obstetrician, an anesthesiologist, a neonatal doctor and the nursing and rehab team who would be handling Leah after the operation. He was impressed with how Dr. Morris was on top of things. Dr. McNeil did a thorough evaluation of Leah and the fetus and assured them the baby at this time was at no risk. They felt much better afterward.

Falcon had just about reached his limit with Eden's petulant attitude. She answered when Leah spoke to her but had very little interaction with her mother. Knowing she was going through an emotional upheaval, Falcon gave her time. But his patience was running thin.

One evening as he was getting ready for bed he heard Eden's agitated voice and he hurried down the hall to see what was wrong. Leah was laying on the bed and Eden was leaning over her, a worried expression on her face.

"Are you okay?" Eden asked.

"Y-yes, I just need a moment. A wet washcloth for my forehead would be nice."

Eden darted into the bathroom and Falcon stepped back out of sight, giving mother and daughter this time alone. He could see that Leah probably had another fainting spell but was okay.

"Does that help?" Eden asked as she placed the washcloth on Leah's forehead.

"Yes, thank you."

"I better get Dad."

"I'm fine, Eden. Just sit with me."

"Okay." Eden sat on the bed next to her mother. "Is it the tumor?"

"I'm sick to my stomach so I think it's the baby."

"It's kind of weird thinking I'll have a brother or sister."

"It's weird for me, too."

"Yeah," Eden muttered. "Tell me what you need and I'll get it."

Leah looked at her daughter. "I just need you not to be so angry with me."

A tear slipped from Eden's eye. "I—I'm sorry I..."

Leah touched Eden's face. "Don't apologize, sweetie, I understand."

After that, things changed drastically. Eden was at her mother's beck and call. Her nurturing nature had finally kicked in and every day it was a pleasure to watch how his daughter changed into the young woman he knew she was.

LEAH WAS TAKING baby steps with her daughter, giving her time to adjust to the new situation. Little by little she was coming around. Eden now talked to her instead of at her, but she still had not called Leah by her name or by "mother." Leah didn't know if that was ever going to happen.

One evening she came out of the bathroom to find Eden standing in her doorway with an arm full of photo albums.

"Are you busy?" Eden asked tentatively.

"No, sweetie. What have you got there?"

"I brought some of my baby pictures in case you wanted to see me when I was a baby and a little girl."

That's what she had in the suitcase that was so heavy. Leah's heart fluttered with excitement. Even though Eden was mad at her she'd still brought the pictures. That said more than words could.

With a quavering voice, she said, "Of course I want to see them, every last one of them. Let's sit on the bed and you can explain each one."

Looking through her daughter's life was a surreal moment because Leah could see her daughter grow. Tears filled her eyes because she knew she would never get those years back. She'd paid dearly for that and she hoped she didn't have to pay any more. She would grab this time with her child and enjoy every moment.

"What the..." Falcon came into the room in pajamas and stared at all the photos on the bed. "So that's what you had in the suitcase?"

"Yeah. I thought...my mother would like to see them."

On impulse Leah leaned over and kissed her daughter's cheek. "She does."

"But, baby, it's late and your mother needs to get her rest."

Eden made a face at him. "Just a few more minutes." She pointed to a picture. "That's my first room where I had to sleep all by myself and I didn't like it one bit. I slept in Dad's room until I was about three and then he said I was getting bigger and needed my own room. We went shopping and bought new furniture and I was excited until Dad turned out the light. Even the night-light didn't help. I cried and cried, but he made me sleep in my room."

Leah glanced at Falcon. "You didn't?"

"Yeah," Eden rambled on, "and when he wouldn't come get me, I grabbed my My Little Pony pillow and blanket and snuck into his room and slept on the floor at the foot of his bed. He almost stepped on me the next morning. But that didn't change his mind. No." Eden shook her head. "Dad said I had to sleep in my room, but I did the same thing again and again."

Falcon sat on the other side of the bed and pushed up against the headboard. "I was determined she was going to sleep in her room, but it didn't come without a battle."

"What did you do?" Leah asked in a breathless voice.

"I had to negotiate. Eden's whole life has been a negotiation. She wanted her own horse, so I told her if she'd sleep in her room, I'd buy her a pony. That did the trick. When she was five, I wanted her to wear dresses to church. She refused. She wanted red boots, so I told her if she would wear a dress, I'd buy the boots. When she was ten—"

"We get it, Dad."

Falcon and Eden had such a good relationship and it warmed Leah's heart. She missed so much, but she wasn't going to dwell on that. Her daughter was here and making an effort. That's what counted. The relationship that they would build now was what mattered the most.

"Okay, baby girl, time to gather up the photos and go to bed."

Leah was surprised that Eden obeyed, but then she figured Eden didn't defy her father too often. Only when it was important, and Leah had a feeling she knew when those times were right.

Eden hugged her dad and then paused, glancing at Leah. "I never know whether to hug you or not."

Leah tried to stop her racing heart to reply. "Always hug me. It means the world to me."

And just like that her daughter reached out and hugged her, and Leah held on with all her strength, never wanting to let go. It made her realize just how valuable each moment was.

After Eden left, Falcon scooted closer to Leah. "I had no idea she had those albums in her suitcase."

"Do you think it means she's starting to forgive me?"

He shrugged. "I don't think it's so much forgiveness, Leah, as it is adjusting. She's had so many years without you and now that you're in her life she's not quite sure what to do."

"Is it the same for you?"

His gaze met hers. "Yeah, something like that."

She fingered the collar of his pajamas. "I can't get used to you in these."

A smile split his face. "I thought I never would. I couldn't walk around in my underwear anymore with a little girl around."

She batted her eyes. "You look quite charming, sir. Like a father in an old sitcom."

"Being a parent changes a man."

"It's a change for the better."

Falcon swung his long legs off the bed, as if the moment was getting too intimate. "I'll take that as a compliment, ma'am. Now it's time for you to go to bed."

She ran her hands up her arms. "Can I ask you a question first?"

"Sure."

"When we were teenagers, did you marry me because you loved me or because I was pregnant?"

His eyebrows knotted together. "What kind of question is that? You know I loved you."

"In my heart, I guess I did, but you didn't say it often and I said it all the time. And when I got pregnant you didn't say, 'I love you so let's get married.' You said, 'We have to get married.'"

He sighed. "Why are you bringing this up now?"

It was going to be hard to explain her feelings, but she had to do her best. "You and Eden can't understand why I didn't come home and I've explained my reasons several times. Guilt for leaving was a big part of it, but I think a part of me thought after so long that you didn't love me anymore. And that maybe the love was all on my part."

"Leah…"

"I'd never felt real love in my life and making love with you seemed to say 'LOVE' in capital letters. But at times I've wondered and I think that doubt made me insecure to come home when I wasn't well."

Then he did something unexpected. He sat beside her, so close she could smell a whiff of tangy soap, sending a charge of excitement through her. He leaned over and kissed the softness of her neck, her jawline and then the corner of her mouth. "You were the only thing I thought about day and night," he whispered. "I didn't look at other girls. As far as I was concerned there were no other girls. You were my girl and my life and I thought I showed you that in every way. If you had doubts..."

The excitement quickly turned to desire and she touched her lips to his, wrapping her arms around his neck. She needed to kiss and hold him and a whole lot more. He deepened the kiss and for a moment they were lost in the flames of bygone days when nothing mattered but the two of them. Memories like wispy puffs of smoke surrounded Leah. She felt his love again for the first time, and she had to wonder if he felt it, too.

"Dad!" Eden hollered from her room.

He drew back slightly, his breath a wave of delicious heat on her skin. "I'm always going to love you and I'm always going to want you. That's just the way I am, but we have to take time now to get to know each other once again and to build a future that we both want."

"Does that mean you're always going to resent what I did?"

"No. It means we have to take time to adjust and not let our emotions cloud our judgments."

"Dad!" Eden hollered again.

Falcon got up and went into his daughter's bedroom.

Leah curled up in bed, not knowing what to feel or what to do. She just had this feeling that Falcon was never going to forgive her.

FALCON AGONIZED OVER his talk with Leah. They couldn't go back as if nothing had happened, and sex wasn't going to solve their problems. He had to remind himself of that from time to time. But he missed that intimacy with her.

He didn't understand why he couldn't say, "I forgive you," and they could move on. It wasn't as if he loved someone else. He'd waited almost eighteen years for Leah to return and now he was as conflicted as Eden.

The relationship between Leah and Eden had changed and he was happy about that. After the ice was broken, so to speak, his daughter seemed to have a need to tell her mother about every little thing in her life and Leah listened avidly. Then Eden discovered she could wear Leah's clothes and shoes. Thus began an adventure like he'd never seen. He always worried about Eden developing her feminine side, but with her mother it became natural.

Then Leah showed her how to use makeup and he hardly recognized his daughter, who always wore jeans and boots and maybe a little lip gloss. She was turning into a woman right before his eyes. A part of him longed for the little girl who slept on the floor at the foot of his bed. But Eden was happier than Falcon had ever seen her.

They had the house to themselves, since Alma had gone to visit her sister, who'd just had knee surgery. Leah wanted to do everything for them, but soon found she couldn't. Somehow it was important to her that she cooked for them. She had dizzy spells, so he and Eden chipped in and made it fun for her. But Falcon worried Leah was getting worse. While she was playing games with Eden sometimes she had to stop because she couldn't see.

Anne was now confined to bed until the baby was born. But she and Leah talked every morning on the phone. Callie and Lissie came to visit and meet Eden. There was a tense moment when Eden realized these young girls, her age, were friends with her mother. But the girls were very friendly and soon Eden warmed up to them.

The days passed quickly with numerous doctor visits, and soon it was the end of October. Leah and the baby continued to do well. He thought it might be good for Eden to go home for a while and that was met with a frown. No way was she leaving her mother now. Each day they drew closer.

Leah's headaches and dizziness grew worse. One night she woke him up.

"Falcon."

He instantly sat up. Since the birth of Eden, he'd been a light sleeper.

"What?"

"I have a terrible headache and when I try to stand up I'm so dizzy I'm afraid I'll fall. Could you please get me the Tylenol out of the bathroom?"

He didn't flip on a light because he knew it would hurt her eyes. The moonlight streaming through the windows provided all the light he needed. He got the medication and brought it back to her with a glass of water. She quickly took it and lay down.

"Is it bad?"

"The worst."

He went back to the bathroom and fixed a cool washcloth and crawled into bed. He gathered her into his arms and placed the washcloth over her eyes.

"Take a couple of deep breaths and relax."

"I can't. The pain is so bad."

"Shh. The medicine will take effect soon."

"I'm afraid the tumor is growing like Dr. Morris predicted."

"We'll call him in the morning," he murmured and kissed the top of her head.

He held her until she drifted back to sleep. A delicate scent of flowers reached him and he sucked in the fragrance like a dying man. She smelled so good and her skin was soft and yielding against his fingertips. Heat radiated from his skin and desire uncurled in his stomach. God, he wanted her, but tonight was not the time.

By morning, Leah was better and decided to wait for her regular visit with Dr. Morris. But in the days that followed they both knew Leah was getting worse. Dr. Morris scheduled an MRI without contrast to check on the tumor. The tumor was now growing, as they'd suspected.

Dr. Morris had them register at the hospital in case of an emergency. He wanted to be prepared and so did they. They soon found out that Leah's insurance would not cover pregnancy and that meant they would have to pay out of pocket for that and the hospital wanted a deposit. Then Falcon remembered that he'd never taken Leah off his insurance policy. He called Quincy to pull the records to find out for sure. Thirty minutes later Quincy called back to tell him Leah was still on the policy and it included pregnancy. It was a big relief.

The days ahead were rough as Leah continued to have

problems. One morning he woke to find her in the bathroom throwing up. He immediately got a washcloth and held her trembling body as she retched.

"Go away, Falcon. I don't want you to see this."

"Hey, we're in this together for better or worse." He sat on the floor holding her, making sure there was no blood in the vomit. He flushed the toilet and continued to hold her, wiping her face until her trembling subsided. Then he picked her up and carried her back to the bed.

"Falcon…"

"Shh. Just get some rest."

"It's too soon. I can't have the surgery now. The baby is only ten weeks."

Falcon worried about that, too. They may have to choose between Leah's life and the baby's. And he knew without even asking her what her choice would be. And in that moment, some of that deep resentment that he still held started to dissipate.

ANNE HAD DELIVERED a healthy baby boy two weeks ago and Leah still hadn't seen him. She was happy for her friends and hoped they would bring the baby soon to see her because going out was out of the question. Her health was deteriorating and she held on to Falcon and Eden just as hard as she could. She didn't know how she ever thought she could handle it alone because the pain was debilitating. They didn't seem to mind cleaning up her vomit or holding her while she cried. She worried now that she was going to lose the baby. Soon she knew Dr. Morris would push for the surgery and she had to be strong to resist. The baby needed more time and she needed more time with her husband and daughter. She had another difficult decision, but this time she

knew she would not make it alone. She'd given up on
Falcon forgiving her. Now she hoped that somewhere
in his heart he could accept her into his life again. By
his caring actions she knew that was a possibility and
she would accept anything he offered. She loved him
that much.

Eden was subdued about the whole thing. She wanted
her mother to be healthy, but she didn't want Leah to be in
pain. What she'd feared was happening: they were watching her suffer. She spent most days going through the
photos. She pulled two photos out that she wanted to keep.
One was of Eden in her red boots and dress and the other
was of Leah and Falcon the day they'd gotten married.

They looked so young and they were without a clue
of what was to come and all the heartache they would
suffer. And it wasn't over.

ANNE BROUGHT THE baby over and Leah was besotted with
the chubby cheeked infant. As she held him, she had to
wonder if she would see the child that she carried. Every
day was a blessing and she counted it as such.

Thanksgiving Day dawned wet and dreary. The
Rebel family was coming and Eden was beside herself. Leah was nervous because she hadn't seen them in
years, but it was a holiday and she hoped she was well
enough to enjoy it. Alma was cooking turkey and dressing and Kate was bringing food, too. Falcon and Eden
had never spent Thanksgiving away from the ranch
and Leah tried to get them to go home for the holiday,
but they refused.

Leah made it downstairs, but she wasn't allowed to do
anything and she really didn't have the energy anyway.

Soon Kate Rebel, her sons, Zane and Grandpa arrived. She met Rachel, Egan's wife, and liked her immediately.

Kate kissed Leah's cheek. "I hope this isn't too much for you."

"No. I wouldn't have it any other way." And just like that the tension from the past disappeared.

Kate looked at her sons. "I expect everyone to behave and act like gentlemen today. This is a nice house and I want it to be that way when we leave."

"Yes, ma'am," echoed around the room.

"Where's the TV?" Paxton asked.

"Right this way." Eden led them toward the den.

"Wait a minute." Falcon stopped them. "I want you to meet Alma. She's the housekeeper and has been taking care of Leah."

They shook hands with the woman and Alma fanned her face. "Oh, my, I haven't been around this many cowboys in my whole life."

"Ah, they're just babies. I'm the real deal." Grandpa thumbed into his chest.

"He is." Eden winked at Alma.

The day turned out to be lively with family, and Leah enjoyed every minute. She didn't know if it was the excitement or what, but she wasn't dizzy and she could see fairly well.

The brothers watched football and yelled and screamed at the TV while the ladies fixed lunch. Grandpa did his best to impress Alma. They ate in the dining room and managed to squeeze around the table.

Eden was in her element with the uncs and Leah saw how much she'd missed them. It was a family day, like it should be, and Leah, for the first time, felt a part of the Rebel family.

THE DAYS OF DECEMBER seemed to drag as Falcon continued to watch Leah grow worse. She was now on bed rest because Dr. Morris was afraid of her falling. Headaches and dizziness were a daily thing and her eyesight continued to decline. Falcon was worried out of his mind because he knew Leah wasn't going to agree to surgery until the baby was a little bigger.

She was now showing and it brought back so many memories of when she was pregnant with Eden. This time he was determined to be there for her every step of the way.

David came over and they talked about their options..

"How many weeks is she now?" David asked.

"Fifteen."

"I think there's a very good chance the baby will survive the surgery. I've seen it many times and there's minimal risk to the baby. Dr. Morris will make the decision. He's on top of this and he'll not let it go one minute longer than it has to. I hope Leah accepts his decision."

"Will there come a time when we have to choose between Leah's life and the baby's?"

David nodded. "Be prepared for that, but it's probably a very slim chance." He looked straight at Falcon. "How are you and Leah doing?"

"We're getting to know each other all over again. I have to be honest, though, it's hard after so many years apart and it's hard for me to accept the reason for our separation. I'm trying, though."

David picked up his briefcase he'd set on the floor. "I brought something over that you might be interested in." He opened his briefcase and pulled out a huge medical folder with Leah's name on it. "Years ago Leah signed medical release forms and asked me to get her records.

She read some of it and gave it back to me saying it was too depressing. I've kept it at my house, but it really belongs to you and Leah. It's interesting reading. It might open your eyes a little."

"Thanks," Falcon said and later carried the folder to his room. He would read it when he had time.

Leah and Eden were in Leah's bedroom and Eden was prancing around in high heels. He stopped for a moment to watch his grown-up daughter. She ruined the model-like walk by giggling. Since his wife and daughter were busy, he decided to take a look at the folder.

As he opened it he saw there were several folders inside the big one: one from the accident, one from rehab and another from plastic surgery and surgery to her legs. There were also pictures from the accident and he didn't recognize the woman who was his wife. Her face was swollen, one ear dangled and an eye bulged out. Her face was covered in blood and his stomach cramped at the pain she must've endured.

He kept flipping through and reading. Notes from the doctors caught his eye:

Patient not expected to make it through the night. Patient a fighter, a survivor.

On and on he read and it was like a story of the time Leah had been away from them. When she woke up from the coma, there were more notes.

Patient awake asking for Eden. Patient calling for Falcon. She has no idea who these people are. A therapist has been called.

The therapist added more notes after Leah knew who Eden and Falcon were.

Patient in agony over leaving her husband and child. When it is suggested she call them, she becomes agitated saying she can't go home until she's well. Feels extreme guilt over her actions.

As he read through all the files, any anger or resentment or doubt that he'd harbored vanished. It was clear to him now. Somewhere in his mind he believed that Leah had forgotten about him as she enjoyed her cushy life in Houston. He could see that wasn't true. He and Eden were always on her mind. Even though he felt she made the wrong decision, he knew Leah and how it must've hurt her not to come home. For the first time he could admit that.

He slammed the files shut. He had to talk to his wife.

"Dad, it's Mama," Eden screamed.

He jumped to his feet and ran to Leah's bedroom. She lay on the floor curled into a ball holding her head, whimpering.

Kneeling beside her, he asked, "What happened?"

"We were having fun and her head started to hurt and now it's really bad," Eden replied. "Do something."

Falcon lifted Leah into his arms and carried her to the bed.

"No, Falcon," Leah moaned. "Leave me alone. I don't want you to see me like this."

"Get a wet washcloth," he ordered Eden.

He brushed back Leah's dark hair. "Take a deep breath. I'm not going anywhere, beautiful lady. I'm in this forever."

Leah rested against him. "She called me Mama."

"Cool, huh?"

He lay on one side of Leah and Eden lay on the other. They turned out the lights and continued to change the washcloth on her forehead until the pain subsided. Together, as a family, they were stronger.

EARLY THE NEXT morning he stirred as the light danced through the windows. He'd made Eden go to her own bed the night before because Leah was resting comfortably. Easing away from his wife, he was careful not to wake her. She needed her rest.

He hurried to his room to shower, shave and get dressed. As he tucked his shirt into his jeans, something niggled him. Leah was limp when he'd moved away from her. But she was asleep. Still, that bothered him. He ran down the hall back into her room.

"Leah," he said, and she didn't respond. He said her name a little louder and still she didn't move. Fear shot up his spine, but he tried to stay focused. He shook her and she lay like a limp doll. *Oh, God!*

He pulled his phone from his pocket with a shaky hand and called 9-1-1. Then he called Dr. Morris and apprised him of the situation. The doctor was already at the hospital and said he would be waiting.

"Eden," he shouted. "Get up."

Eden dragged in with her hair all over her face. "What?"

"I need you to remain calm."

Eden brushed her hair from her eyes. "Calm? I'm barely awake."

"Listen to me. We don't have a lot of time. Your mother is not waking up and I've called an ambulance."

Color drained from his daughter's face. "W-what? No!" She ran to the bed and stroked Leah's hair. "Mama, wake up. It's me."

A lump formed in Falcon's throat. He pulled his daughter away and held her face in his hands. "I need you to remain calm. Understand?"

Tears filled Eden's eyes as she nodded.

"Go downstairs and wake Alma so the ambulance doesn't scare her and then open the front door for the paramedics."

"O-okay." Eden shot from the room as the blare of a siren echoed in the distance.

He sat by Leah and stroked her hair from her face as Eden had. "Can you hear me, beautiful lady? Wake up. Please. I have so much to tell you. You were right. I still had resentment in my heart over you leaving me, but I don't anymore. I love you. I'm always going to love you no matter what you do or what you say. That's a given. I hope you can hear me. Leah…"

Voices and loud footsteps echoing on the stairs stopped him. He kissed her warm lips and stood, ready to face whatever this day would hold, hoping he had that much strength.

FALCON RODE IN the ambulance with Leah. That's when he realized he didn't have his boots on, just his socks. That didn't matter. The only thing that mattered was Leah.

Things happened fast once they reached the hospital. She was taken directly to the OR where Dr. Morris and his team waited. After he examined Leah, he came out to talk to Falcon.

"She's in a coma," the doctor said. "They're prepping her for surgery. Dr. McNeil's team is here and they will monitor the fetus. The anesthesiologist you spoke to is also here and getting ready. We've all been on alert for this and we're prepared to do our very best."

"Is she going to make it?"

"There are no guarantees, but we're all highly qualified in our fields and she will get the best medical care. Go get breakfast, call your family. Do something besides sit here, because it's going to take a while."

"How long?"

"Three to four hours, or possibly more. We have two patients to monitor and it's going to be a slow go. Just be patient and pray for the best."

The doctor turned and then swung back. "This was around her neck and I wanted to give it to you personally in case it got lost." He placed a locket and chain in Falcon's hand.

As the doctor walked off, Falcon opened the locket and inside was a photo of him and Eden. He gazed at it in shock, so many thoughts running through his mind, but one remained true: she held them close to her heart. Always.

He stood there with the locket in his hand and felt as if his world had come to an end one more time—and this time he felt it might be for good.

Unable to deal with all the pain and guilt inside him he ran to the elevators and went down to the ground floor and out the doors. Once outside, he started to run and kept running. He wasn't sure where he was going. He just needed the exercise to clear his mind. He ran and ran until his lungs were so tight he had to stop. Sinking onto a bench, he gulped in air.

He might lose Leah today and she wouldn't know he'd forgiven her. That kept eating at him, but he had to pull himself together for their daughter. His cell buzzed and he pulled it out of his pocket.

"Dad, where are you? Where's Mama?"

"I'll be right there." Getting up, he realized he still had on just his socks and his feet ached from running in them. He hadn't even noticed until now.

He found Eden and Alma in the OR waiting room. Eden jumped up when she saw him.

"They said Mama was in surgery."

"Yes. Dr. Morris is removing the tumor."

"What about the baby?"

"They're looking out for the baby. We just have to wait and see."

Eden held up a rosary. "We have to pray, Dad. Alma gave me a rosary and she's teaching me how to pray on it. I have to believe everything is going to be okay."

When had his daughter become so grown up?

Alma held up a bag. "I brought your boots and Stetson, Mr. Cowboy."

"Thank you." He sat down to put them on and his body relaxed. Leah had to be okay.

Alma went to get coffee since they hadn't had any that morning. She brought back coffee and sweet rolls, but Falcon couldn't eat. The thought of food turned his stomach, as did what they were doing to Leah's head.

Time dragged. One hour faded into another and then another. He paced the hall, but nothing helped.

The sound of boots echoed loudly in the hallway. Eden ran to the door. Falcon followed her and saw all his brothers, his mother and Grandpa walking toward them.

Eden shot out of the room to meet them. She kissed Grandpa's cheek. "Have you missed me?"

"You bet I have. Quincy won't buy me pizza."

"I'm not going into town every day and buying you pizza," Quincy stated. "It's not good for you anyway."

"Don't you worry. Cupcake'll buy it for me."

The nurses were staring at all the cowboys and Falcon motioned for them to come into the room. They squeezed in and Paxton and Phoenix had to sit on the floor, but they were there. That's what counted, because he needed his family today. All of them.

But he had to ask, "How did y'all know?"

"Eden called early this morning," his mother replied. "We're not letting you go through this alone."

"Who's running the ranch?"

"Jericho," Quincy answered. "And Gabe's helping him." Gabe was their uncle and had been raised with them. Their grandmother had died and Kate had refused to let her brother go into foster care. Gabe was a lawyer in Horseshoe.

"Jericho said not to worry about the McCrays causing trouble while everyone is away," Egan said. "He'll be riding the fence lines to make sure and I don't think any of the McCrays want to come face-to-face with him in any kind of fight."

Falcon doubted that, too.

"Have you heard anything, son?" his mom asked.

"No, and it's been over three hours." He got to his feet. "I think I'll go ask at the desk again."

The nurse at the desk said Leah was still in surgery and Falcon grew restless. He had to hear something soon. He went back to the room and listened to Paxton and Phoenix talk about the National Finals Rodeo in Vegas that they'd participated in in early December. Their voices went right over his head.

Another hour passed and the family and Alma went

to get lunch. David and Anne arrived and assured him Dr. Morris was the best surgeon and they were positive for good results. Falcon hoped that with all his heart. The family returned and the waiting went on.

Just when Falcon's nerves were about to snap Dr. Morris stood in the doorway. Falcon was immediately on his feet.

"Could I speak to you for a moment, please?"

"Daddy…"

"Stay here," he told Eden. "I'll be right back." But his stomach churned as he followed Dr. Morris into the hall. Dr. McNeil stood there waiting.

"The surgery went well," Dr. Morris said. "I was able to resect and remove the complete tumor. I feel I got it all. We'll do more tests and see how she does in the next few days."

Relief surged through his body and it took a moment for him to catch his breath. Leah was alive.

"And the baby remained stable," Dr. McNeil added. For some reason Falcon sensed a *but* coming really fast.

"Everything is good, then? Leah is fine and so is the baby?" And then it hit him. "Can she see?"

Dr. Morris removed his surgical cap. "Yes. Leah is in recovery and she's awake. We'll move her to SICU soon and you can see her there."

He looked from one doctor to the other. "But something is wrong. I can feel it."

"There is always a risk of complications." Dr. Morris twisted the cap in his hand and Falcon wanted to snatch it from him because he knew something bad was coming.

"What kind of complications?"

At the doctor's somber expression apprehension

coiled through Falcon. "Leah has gone back in her mind almost eighteen years. She thinks she's seventeen and pregnant with her daughter."

"What?"

"I believe it's only temporary, but it will take time for her brain to heal. I've seen this before and it just takes time. Trust me."

"Trust you? My wife is stuck in limbo and you want me to trust you? I trusted you with the surgery." Falcon's voice rose in anger.

"I'm sorry, Mr. Rebel. I warned Leah of the risks and I warned you, too. I'm not giving up and you shouldn't, either. Just be patient."

"When can I see her?" His voice was as cold as the icy chills running down his back.

"My team will keep monitoring the baby," Dr. McNeil said. "So far there are no complications there. Just stay strong."

How strong was he supposed to be?

Chapter Fifteen

A time to pray...

Falcon took a moment to calm himself. Gulping in a deep breath, he walked into the waiting room and told his daughter and the family the disturbing news.

Eden sobbed into his chest. "Daddy, no."

He held her. "We have to be strong for your mother. The doctor said it could be temporary. You stay here with Grandma and the uncs. I'm going to go see if they'll let me talk to her."

Eden wiped away tears. "I want to come, too. I want her to know that I'm there."

"Maybe later." He kissed her forehead. "Right now I have to find out how bad your mother is. Stay here."

Falcon strolled from the room, glad his daughter didn't insist. His strength was waning and he didn't know if he could fight her on this. He asked at the desk where SICU was and made his way to the elevators. Quincy got on with him.

"There's no need for you to come," he told his brother.

"You don't need to do this alone," was Quincy's response.

Falcon didn't say anything else. He was too emotional to be rational.

At the nurse's desk in SICU he asked to see his wife.

"I'm sorry, sir. You can only see her during visiting hours," he was told.

That's when his calm snapped. "I want to see my wife now!"

The tone of his voice shocked the nurse, who just stared up at him with wide eyes. He didn't know what would've happened if Dr. Morris hadn't walked up.

"I got it, Janice," he said to the nurse, and motioned for Falcon to follow him. Quincy waited at the nurse's desk.

Leah was in one of the rooms that circled a big nurses' station. He went inside with Dr. Morris and froze at the sight of his wife. Leah lay in the bed very pale and still. A bandage was wrapped around her head and secured under her chin. They'd shaved her head. Tubes seemed to be everywhere, as did monitors. One of the monitors was for the baby, and Falcon could see the heartbeat. All the anger left him at the tiny miracle. He stepped closer to the bed as two nurses checked the monitors.

Leah's skin was almost white and her eyes looked as if she had two black eyes, indicating she'd been through a tremendous ordeal. His breath caught in his throat and he tried to breathe normally.

Dr. Morris was on the other side of the bed. "Leah, can you hear me?"

Leah moved her head from side to side, as if trying to wake up.

"Someone is here to see you," Dr. Morris added.

Leah's eyelashes fluttered and then her eyes opened and focused on Falcon. She smiled slightly.

"O-oh…Mr. Rebel."

Mr. Rebel. Leah never called him that and for a moment he was lost for words.

Dr. Morris indicated for him to say something.

He swallowed. "How are you?"

"Fine." Her voice was low, but he heard it. "Is Falcon with you?"

Then it dawned on him. Leah thought he was John Rebel, his father. It took a moment for him to gather his thoughts and he had no idea how to respond. Dr. Morris motioned him out of the room. He took one last look at his wife and followed.

Outside in the hall, he raked a hand through his hair and looked at Dr. Morris. "She's not any better. She thinks I'm my dad. How am I supposed to handle this?"

"I've studied the brain extensively but it still holds many mysteries to doctors. I could spout a lot of medical terms and theories to you, but simply Leah has gone back in her mind to a happier time. That's where she can function right now. I promise you, just give her brain time to heal and you'll have her back, but it's going to take a lot of patience. In the meantime, the baby is doing well and Dr. McNeil and her team will continue to make sure the baby has the best chance possible."

"What am I supposed to tell my daughter? Leah doesn't even know who she is now. She doesn't know who I am. That's horrific to us. We just got her back."

"I'm sorry, Mr. Rebel, but rest assured Leah will get the best possible care. Please, please be patient."

"I don't have much choice."

"Your visits will help to stimulate her brain, so it would help to talk to her."

"She doesn't know who I am."

Dr. Morris touched Falcon's shoulder. "It doesn't matter who she thinks you are. She needs to talk to someone she's familiar with."

"I'm so frustrated right now I don't know if I can."

"You will. From the little I know about you, Mr. Rebel, you're not giving up."

No, a Rebel never gave up, Falcon thought as he made his way to Quincy.

"Would you like me to stay for a while?" Quincy asked.

"No, Eden and I have to figure out a way to deal with this. And you need to run Rebel Ranch while I'm away because I'm not sure when I'll be returning."

"Okay, but if you need anything, you know my number."

"Thanks, brother. Right now I need a miracle for Leah, me, Eden and the baby."

THE NEXT FEW days were some of the hardest of Falcon's life—right up there with the days after his dad had died. He took one day at a time and did his best. Every day he and Eden went to the hospital. It was extremely difficult, because Eden wasn't allowed to see her mother. It was difficult for him, too. Leah got better with each day, but she still thought she was seventeen years old and pregnant.

He wanted Eden to return to the ranch. There was nothing she could do at the hospital and it was two days before Christmas. After much discussion and tears, Quincy came to Houston to pick her up.

One day turned into another and nothing changed, except Leah was moved to a regular room. He had several meetings with Dr. Morris. Nothing changed there, either. Leah was having trouble walking and a therapist was working with her. The doctor only suggested patience and that was starting to get on Falcon's nerves.

The new year arrived, one week soon became two, and it was getting close to Eden's eighteenth birthday. Leah showed no signs of regaining her memory. Each visit with her was pure torture. She continued to think of him as John Rebel. She never questioned why his father was visiting her and not Falcon. And she never questioned the bandage on her head. Or why she was in the hospital. Or the therapist. She just went through the motions. Dr. Morris asked that he not upset her with questions. So he didn't.

He walked into her room, as he did every day, and she said the same thing. "Hi, Mr. Rebel. Is Falcon with you?" Some days it varied, but it was basically the same response.

Today she was sitting in a chair, staring out the window. All her tubes and monitors had been removed. Her color was much better and he knew her health was improving. It was her mind that was locked in the past and he began to despair of that ever changing.

"No, he isn't," he replied.

"That's okay. I know he's working hard to prepare us a home."

He always went along with everything she said. "Yes, he's very busy."

"I can't wait for us to move into our own home. Thank you for letting us have the old house. I know it's a lot of work to move everything y'all have stored there, but it's perfect for us."

She'd mentioned the old house before and he never realized how important it was to her to have a home.

They'd made plans, but Falcon had never got around to completing them. Once again he felt as if he had failed her.

As if reading his thoughts, she said, "I've never had my own home. When we lived in Alabama, we rented, and then my mom died and my dad and I moved to Texas to live with my aunt. I've always wanted my own place. A place I could call home. And now I will have that with Falcon and our new baby. I'm so happy."

The light in her eyes reflected her feelings and how he wished he could go back and be more aware of her emotions at that time. He'd kept putting off cleaning out the house because he'd worked from sunup to sundown and he hadn't had any energy left.

She placed her hand over her swelling stomach. "I know Falcon wants a boy. He won't say that, but I just can't see him raising a girl. Can you?"

Falcon twisted the Stetson in his hand. "Oh, I think he would love a little girl to death."

"If it's a boy, we're going to name him John. We're undecided on a girl's name. I like Eden, but Falcon wants to name her Jessie or Josie or something like Belle."

"I like Eden."

"Do you? I like it, too."

Leah looked out the window and there was silence for a moment. Then she glanced at him. "I'm sorry you're disappointed in us."

He didn't have a clue as to what she was talking about so he remained quiet, hoping she would elaborate. When she didn't, he said, "I'm not disappointed."

"But you wish we'd been more careful about getting pregnant. I know we're young, but we're in love and we can make it work. I just…"

"What?"

"Sometimes I feel as if Falcon married me because I'm pregnant. He has a hard time saying I love you. I know he does, but sometimes I wonder."

A chill settled over Falcon. It was a surreal moment to get a glimpse of her feelings back then, something she hadn't voiced to him at the time.

He gauged his words carefully, trying to say them as his father would. "I know my boy pretty well and I can honestly say he loves you with all his heart. Yes, you're going to be parents at a very young age, but Kate and I were young, too."

She touched her chest. "Thank you, Mr. Rebel. Could you do me a favor, please?"

"Anything."

"Could you let Falcon off early so he can come visit?"

I'm here. Please recognize me. Look into my face and see your husband. Please, Leah.

"Sure," he replied when she kept staring at him.

"Thank you," was all she said, and he left the room because he couldn't say anything else. The visits were getting too hard, but he didn't know what else he could do until she regained her memory.

Chapter Sixteen

A time to cry...

Eden's birthday arrived and Falcon decided to go home for the day so one of her parents would be there to celebrate. He had Quincy searching for a truck for her and he'd found one in Temple. It would be delivered and Falcon wanted to be there to see her face. It was a white four-wheel-drive with all the extras. And Grandpa and the uncs had bought her a horse trailer to go with it.

He'd never been away this long from Rebel Ranch and he yearned for home, but not as much as he yearned for his wife to get well.

There was no change in Leah that morning, so he headed home and was on the ranch in time for breakfast. He called to let his mother know he was coming, and the house was festive with balloons and banners and streamers for his daughter's birthday.

Falcon slipped outside to breathe in the fresh country air he'd missed so much. Home—there was no place like it. He headed for the barn to saddle up Titan. It had been too long since he'd been on a horse. He whistled and Titan galloped for the barn. Within minutes he had a saddle on him and rode for the open outdoors. He gave

Titan his lead and they flew over brittle coastal patches and dried weeds. He slowed the horse as they reached the woods. But he kept riding, checking cattle to see how the herds were doing. The salt and mineral blocks were out and round bales of hay were in each pasture. The ranch was doing fine without him.

The cold north wind blew against him and he buttoned his sheepskin coat. His nose was cold, but it felt good to be outdoors again. For some reason he rode toward the McCray property and saw Gunnar and Malachi near the fence. Their horses stood some distance away.

He rode to about twenty feet from them. Gunnar looked up. "Well, Rebel, you made it home. I heard in town that Leah returned, but she has a tumor or something and you've been by her bedside."

Falcon didn't show any emotion on his face. "You heard correctly."

Gunnar shook his head. "Man, Leah didn't deserve that."

Falcon didn't miss the fence cutter that Malachi was holding behind his back. In a neighborly spirit, he said, "When are you going to stop cutting our fences? When is this feud going to end? Life is too short to keep this up."

"We will never stop!" Gunnar shouted. "Your dad killed our uncle."

"But that's not our fight. It's time to let it go."

Gunnar swung into the saddle, as did Malachi. Still trying to hide the fence cutter. "Never. You're getting weak, Rebel."

"You have kids, Gunnar. What would you do if someone shot them…in cold blood?"

"Shut up."

Seemed he'd hit a nerve so he thought he'd give them

a warning. "While I'm away Jericho will be keeping an eye on the fences and he's not near as nice as I am. If he sees a fence cutter in your hand near the fence, like Malachi has now, he'll slit your throat and feed you to the buzzards piece by piece. You see, Jericho has nothing to lose and he's fiercely loyal to the Rebels."

Gunnar jerked his horse's bridle and he and Malachi galloped away.

Falcon nudged Titan closer to the fence to make sure it wasn't cut. It wasn't. He'd gotten there just in time. He'd have to tell Jericho and the brothers to keep a close eye on this area of the ranch.

When he made it back to the house, everyone had arrived, including Egan and Rachel, his uncle Gabe, Gabe's wife, Lacey, and their daughter, Emma. The whole family was together to celebrate, even Jericho.

After lunch, they all went outside for the big surprise. Quincy had the truck and trailer parked near the back door and Eden just stared.

She smiled at Falcon. "Is that mine?"

Quincy put an arm around her shoulders. "Yes, ma'am. The truck is from your dad and mom. The trailer is from the uncs and Grandpa."

"But Grandpa gave me the silver dollars."

"Now don't go quibbling about what Grandpa gives you. Just enjoy it." Grandpa took her hand and led her toward the truck and trailer. "Let's see if you can drive it with the trailer attached."

"No sweat."

Zane jumped into the passenger seat and for the next thirty minutes Eden backed that trailer up to everything imaginable on the ranch, smiling as if she'd won the lottery. She was happy for this moment in time. But the sadness lurked just beyond the surface.

Seeing how happy Eden was to be home with the family, he talked her into staying. It wasn't easy, but in the end she gave in. He wanted her to enjoy some of her senior year and be with her friends. And he promised to call the first moment there was a change in Leah.

There was a sad moment as he hugged his daughter goodbye, but he knew it was the right decision. The sadness was dragging them both down and Eden needed to be away from the hospital for a while.

But he missed her in that big house in Houston. He hoped Leah's condition would turn around soon.

Becoming wary that Leah would ever regain her memory, he scheduled an appointment with Dr. Morris. As always the doctor pulled out books and graphs to explain Leah's brain and what was happening.

Falcon waved a hand. "I don't want to see those again. All I know is Leah is not regaining her memory. Her brain should have healed by now. I want an honest answer. Is Leah ever going to regain her memory? Is she ever going to remember me or our daughter?"

"I've seen things happen with the brain that can't be easily explained. This is one of them. My team keeps a close eye on everything she does. She's in a repetitive mood. She does the same thing every day. I want to shake that up, but I'm waiting because of the baby. Right now the baby is our top priority. Until she gives birth, I can't use any aggressive measures. But rest assured I have every faith she will regain her memory."

But will she remember that she loves me? There it was. That's what was bothering him. When Leah woke up would she see the world differently? Would she see him differently? Finally he asked the doctor because he had to know.

"I have every faith that Leah's emotions and feelings will be the same, so please stop worrying."

"No offense, Doc, but this has been a nightmare."

"I know. Leah is lucky to have you here. She will need you when she regains her memory. After the baby is born, I will try some aggressive treatments to stimulate her synapses. But I'm counting on the delivery to do more than I can. The pain of childbirth may change something in her brain."

Falcon could do nothing else but trust the doctor. But his faith and trust were waning.

He talked to Eden about three times a day and he'd made the right decision in insisting she stay home. She was back in school and doing well, but of course she missed her mother.

The days seemed to never end and the ranch was the last thing on his mind. But the brothers were handling the winter months and he was proud of the way they had stepped up, making sure the cattle were closely watched and fed.

He was beginning to wonder if the nightmare would ever end.

ONE MORNING IN early March he woke up around 4 a.m. Something bothered him and he couldn't explain it. All he could think was that Leah needed him. He got up, dressed and headed for the hospital.

As he got off the elevator, his cell buzzed. He immediately answered. "Mr. Rebel, this is Dr. McNeil's PA. She asked that you come to the hospital immediately."

"I'm here." As the words left his mouth, Leah's door

opened and she was pushed out on a stretcher. Dr. McNeil and several members of her team were there. "What's going on?"

"I'm sorry, Mr. Rebel, Leah is hemorrhaging and we have to get her to surgery immediately to do a C-section. The baby's pulse is very low and we don't have a choice. We have to go. You can wait in the waiting room."

An invisible balled fist slammed into his chest. Leah was losing the baby. Oh, God, no. No! He walked into her room and sank to the floor, leaning his back against the wall. He'd been waiting for something, but not this. She'd fought so hard for the baby and now… Tears rolled from his eyes and all his strength pooled into a valley of tears around his heart. This was too much even for him. He wiped away another tear and tried to gain control, but strong men sometimes cried, too, even if they were a Rebel. He drew up his knees and cried like he'd never cried before. He never allowed himself that luxury when his dad had died. But now he couldn't control it. Hard sobs shook his body.

After a few minutes, he got to his feet and wiped away the last of the tears. For his wife and daughter he regained his composure. The cell phone was still in his hand and he called Quincy.

Quincy's sleepy voice answered. "What is it?"

"Bring Eden to Houston. They've taken Leah into surgery. I think she's losing the baby and Eden needs to be here. I don't want her driving by herself."

"I'm on it. Don't worry. I'll get her there just as soon as I can."

"Thanks, brother."

Falcon made his way to the surgery area, but he couldn't sit. He paced the hall outside the big double doors. It was too soon—eleven weeks too soon. The baby didn't have much of a chance. The nurse offered him coffee and he gladly accepted it, waiting for Dr. McNeil to come out and tell him the news. This wait was like nothing he'd ever experienced before because no matter what happened he'd have to be strong enough to handle it. And he didn't know if he could.

Dr. Morris arrived and went into surgery. Maybe, just maybe, Leah might regain her memory. But then, how did he tell her the baby was gone? He continued to pace because his thoughts were torturing him.

Finally, Dr. McNeil came out, still in scrubs. Blood was on the front of her clothes and Falcon swallowed the lump in his throat.

"Did she lose the baby?" he asked before she could say a word.

Dr. McNeil shook her head. "No, but it was close. If we had been five minutes later the baby would've died. The umbilical cord was tied around his neck, but you have a new baby son in the neonatal unit. He weighs three pounds one ounce and they're checking him over."

"He?" Falcon's knees buckled and he reached out to brace himself on the wall. They hadn't wanted to know the sex of the baby until the birth.

"Yes. We were lucky that Leah started to hemorrhage and that the nurse noticed the blood on the bed. That saved the baby from being stillborn. You got lucky, Mr. Rebel."

Lucky? Was she kidding?

"The nurse will direct you to the neonatal unit. Dr. Young will take over now. He is a great doctor, so you don't have to worry. Your son is in very good hands. Dr. Morris is with Leah, so he'll be out to talk to you soon." She held out her hand. "Good luck, Mr. Rebel. I know this has been an ordeal, but you're due for some good news."

"Thank you," he replied, shaking her hand.

Falcon's heart pounded so fast that his chest hurt, but in a good way. They had a son. The baby was okay. Small, but okay. For a moment he stood there giving thanks for a son who had been given a chance, the way Leah had wanted. Now Leah had to survive this, too. But he knew it was still touch and go for both of them. He would remain strong, as always, and as the doctor had said they were due for some good news.

Falcon was torn about where to go—to the neonatal unit or to wait for Dr. Morris. He figured his son was being attended to so he waited. Soon the doctor came out.

"They're taking her to Recovery and I will be there when she wakes up. I'm hoping for the best."

"You mean...?"

"Yes, I'm praying there's a change in her memory. You can check on your son and then meet me in SICU. She will wake up in about an hour."

Falcon vigorously shook the man's hand. "I'm going to see my son and I'll see you in an hour. If she wakes up sooner, you know my number."

The doctor's lips twitched into a smile, something Falcon felt he never did. "I have it memorized."

Falcon headed for the elevators. It opened and Eden and Quincy got off. Eden ran to him.

"Daddy, did Mom lose the baby?"

Falcon grabbed her and hugged her so tight she probably couldn't breathe. "You have a baby brother and he's in the neonatal unit. He's very small and not out of the woods, but he's alive."

"Oh, Daddy." Eden began to cry. "And Mama?"

"She's in recovery and the doctors are hoping for the best and we have to do the same. Now let's go see the new addition to our family."

Nothing prepared Falcon for the sight of his tiny son. He was hooked up to tubes and needles and monitors in an incubator, or a warming bed as the nurse called it. But Falcon saw his little chest rising and falling. He was breathing. He was alive. Tears stung his eyes once again but this time he was in total control. They'd been given a miracle. Now he waited to find out about Leah.

A man came out of the unit dressed in scrubs. "I'm Dr. Steven Young. I met you in Dr. McNeil's office."

"Yes. How is my son?"

"He's a preemie, but a fighter. We have a lot of work ahead of us. Later, I will allow you in to touch and hold him. I like the parents to have contact as soon as possible so the baby will form a connection to you. You'll have to put on a gown."

"No problem. I'm sure his mother will want to touch him, too."

Eden poked Falcon in the ribs. "And my daughter, too."

"Family is the best medicine for preemies. They respond to it and I'm sure he'd be happy to get to know his big sister."

"Thank you," Eden replied.

"Mr. Rebel." Falcon turned to see one of Dr. Morris's team behind him. "Your wife is coming around and Dr. Morris wants you in SICU."

"Stay with Quincy," Falcon said to his daughter. "I'll

come back as soon as I can. Keep an eye on your little brother."

Falcon walked as fast as he could to the same unit he had so many months ago and once again he was holding his breath for good results. He was shown into the room. Dr. Morris and two other members of his team were standing around Leah's bed.

Monitor lines were attached to her head and her chest and there was an IV in her arm. Once again she was pale, so pale. She lay still and motionless and his stomach gave way to a foreboding feeling. Was she okay?

Dr. Morris motioned him forward. "Talk to her about anything so she can hear your voice, a familiar voice."

He reached for her limp hand and caressed it. "Hey, beautiful lady. I love you. Open those gorgeous eyes. Just wake up. That's all I want you to do. Can you hear me, Leah? Can you hear me?" He kept talking, saying anything that came into his head, but Leah remained still and unresponsive. Anger shot through him and he motioned to the doctor to meet him outside.

"What's going on?" he demanded. "Why isn't she waking up?"

"Just be—"

"Don't tell me to be patient. I've had enough of that. Just tell me why my wife is not waking up."

"She's lost a lot of blood. Give her time. She's been through—"

"I know what she's been through," Falcon said, cutting him off. "I've been here every second, every minute for months experiencing what she's been through so I don't want to hear that again. You wanted me to trust you and now I'm wondering why I ever did. My wife is in limbo and I get the feeling she's going to stay there."

"Mr. Rebel…"

"No, I don't want to hear anything else you have to say. I want my wife back. Bottom line. Until that happens…"

A hand touched his shoulder and he swung around to see Quincy and Eden standing there. "Calm down," Quincy said.

Falcon turned and walked down the hall to a chair and sank into it. Eden sat beside him. "Daddy, she'll wake up. She has to. I'm going to keep believing. What are you gonna do?"

He ran his hands up his face in despair, but his daughter's words brought him back from the edge. He expelled a deep breath. "I'm gonna wait forever, baby girl."

Chapter Seventeen

A time to live...

For the next couple of days Falcon sat by his wife's bed-side, talking to her, but Leah remained unresponsive. His emotions were all over the place, but he wouldn't lose hope. He managed his temper and his daughter kept him grounded.

Leah had been moved to a private room and he stayed there with her. He shaved and showered in her bathroom and slept with his head on her bed. The nurses brought him food. He wasn't hungry. They brought him a re-cliner, but he still slept with his head on her bed. He had to be close. She would know it and wake up. That was all he could think.

The only time he left was to go to the neonatal unit to visit his son, his very tiny son. He was perfectly formed, but so small. He trembled when he held his son for the first time and tears welled up in his eyes. He was al-most afraid to breathe in case he hurt him. Touching his child—feeling his heartbeat—made Falcon realize what a gift the baby was, and he prayed that Leah would get to see him soon.

Eden kept a vigil by the baby. They let her in regularly and she was forming a connection to her brother. Quincy stayed in Houston to be with them and Falcon insisted that Eden go to the house at night so she could rest. She kept Alma's rosary in her pocket and Falcon admired her faith and courage.

David and Anne visited, as did Alma. His mother and brothers came also, but there still was no change in Leah. The baby kept improving and that was a blessing he clung to.

The days once again ran into each other and there seemed no end. His beautiful wife was lost to him and he couldn't bring her back. Not even "I love you" was enough. The future looked bleak, but Falcon held on with all the strength he had.

IT WAS DARK and Leah couldn't see. She tried to open her eyes, but her eyelids were so heavy. A lethargic feeling was pulling her down. Where was she? Fear gripped her and she fought against the dark place. She would not go there. She had to wake up. Then she heard a voice.

"Leah, can you hear me? Please, wake up. I love you. Can you hear me?"

Yes, she could hear his voice. *Falcon*. Was he in the dark place, too? No. He wasn't, she was sure. She had to fight for the light. Where was the light? The darkness gathered around her, pulling her down, down, down.

"Leah, I'm here. Come back to me."

She moved her head and groaned, fighting to get nearer the voice. If she could just see Falcon, the darkness would not claim her. Her heart raced. She could feel it beating frantically in her chest. *Falcon, I'm coming*. With pure will she forced the darkness away and a light appeared in all its brilliance. And then she was able to open her eyes. The brightness blinded her for a second. But she saw the man with his head on her bed. *Falcon.* He was there!

She tried to pick up her hand, but it was heavy, too. Falcon's presence gave her strength and she inched her fingers over to his arm and touched him. He jumped back, startled.

He stared at her. His gaze mixed with fear and hope. "Leah." His voice was hoarse and she tried to speak, but her throat was dry.

"Leah," he said again, getting to his feet. "Can you see me?"

"Y-yes."

"Who am I?"

She thought that was a strange question, but she replied, "Falcon, my husband."

"Thank God." Tears filled his eyes and it shook her. She'd never seen him cry. He pushed a button and a nurse came into the room. She was in a hospital was her immediate thought. She frowned at the pain.

Dr. Morris rushed in and he asked stupid questions and she didn't understand what was going on. She just wanted Falcon and they seemed to have pushed him away.

"Falcon," she said.

"He's right here," Dr. Morris said. "He's been here for months and he's not leaving now. We just want to check you over so be patient with us."

The doctor shined a light in her eyes and asked her to follow it. She relaxed and answered questions she thought were even stranger. "Is the tumor gone?"

"Yes," Dr. Morris replied.

For the first time she realized her stomach ached. She

was able to raise her hand and place it on her stomach, which was flat. *Oh, no!* "The baby."

Falcon pushed through the nurses. "No, honey. The baby is fine. He's in the neonatal unit. You can see him soon."

"What?" It didn't make sense. She was just a few weeks pregnant. "That can't be true. Don't lie to me."

Falcon kissed her forehead. "I have a long story to tell you, but believe me when I say we have a son."

"A son?"

"Yes, Eden is with him and we're waiting for you to get well. We've been waiting for a long time, beautiful lady. Keep looking at me with those green eyes and everything is going to be okay."

Then he told her a story she could barely believe. "I thought I was seventeen and pregnant with Eden?"

"Yes."

"What month is it?"

"April."

Tears filled her eyes at what had happened. She'd missed so much and had caused him and Eden so much more pain, but she wasn't going to blame herself this time. She was going to accept this precious gift she'd been given.

"I want to see our baby."

"Sorry, Leah," Dr. Morris spoke up. "We want to make sure you're okay before that happens. Maybe later this afternoon."

Falcon pulled out his phone. "I have the next best thing." He tapped his fingers over the screen. "Remember the baby is a preemie. I just want you to be prepared." He showed her a photo. "This is your daughter and son. Eden's taking very good care of him."

Her hand shook as she touched the screen, her eyes glued to the two people on it. "Oh. They're so beautiful." She couldn't help it. Tears trickled from her eyes and she began to cry with joy.

"Hey, hey." Falcon gathered her into his arms, tubes and all.

"I'm so happy."

Falcon kissed her cheek and then pulled the locket from his pocket. Clasping it around her neck, he said, "Rest, beautiful lady, soon everything you ever wanted is going to happen. I promise you, and you know how I know that?"

"No."

He looked into her eyes. "Because I've lost all the resentment that I held in my heart over you leaving me. I love you and I'll love you to the day I die. And beyond."

Staring at her husband, Leah realized the fear that she'd lived with for eighteen years was gone. She now knew beyond a shadow of a doubt that Falcon loved her. He'd married her because he loved her, not because she was pregnant. She could see that now. It was so clear. She didn't understand how she was so positive now, but maybe heartache and pain had opened her heart. Or maybe it was just Falcon and his love that she felt to her very soul.

"Oh, Falcon. I love you, too."

"Good, because it's time for us to live. It's time for us to have a life with our two beautiful children."

She reached up and touched his face. "We got a miracle."

"Yes, we got a miracle."

Epilogue

A time to love...

Falcon woke up to the sound of voices—his favorite female voices: his wife's and daughter's. Glancing at the clock, he saw it was after seven. Leah had let him sleep because he'd been up with the baby last night. She got up during the week and he did over the weekends.

He quickly slipped into jeans and a T-shirt, ready to spend time with his family. In the doorway to the kitchen, he paused at the most beautiful sight in the world to him. Leah was cooking breakfast and the baby lay in a carrier on the table. Obviously he'd just been fed because he was in a good mood, making bubbly cooing sounds to his sister.

It was late August and they were finally home. His eyes stayed on his wife. She had blossomed in the past few months. Her hair was growing back and it was like a dark attractive cap on her head. She wore jean capris and a knit top and looked Eden's age. After all that Leah had been through, she was still the most gorgeous woman he'd ever seen and she always would be.

The days after Leah had woken up hadn't been easy. She had to regain her strength and he'd filled in the blanks about her memory. She still had some memory she couldn't recall, but they were okay with that. She was alive.

The baby stayed in the hospital for two months before he could come home. It was then they'd decided to return to Rebel Ranch to start their life the way they should have years ago. Leah worried at first about postpartum depression, but they were so happy and confident in their love that this time it never happened. She was not afraid of the baby or afraid she might hurt it. She now knew she would never do that. And to this day he believed love had brought them through.

Leah had signed over the house in Houston to the Thornwall estate and Callie and Lissie were going to live in it instead of a dorm. Alma stayed in the house, which was a condition of Leah's.

They left the baby only once and that was to see Eden graduate high school. As a surprise, Leah came on stage to hand her daughter her diploma. Then the two of them cried like babies. It was another moment in their lives they wouldn't forget.

Eden had told her uncles about Leah wanting her own home, so Elias and Quincy had moved out of the old house and in with Grandpa. Under Eden's direction, they had the place repainted and fixed up. Leah was beside herself when she saw it. They had their own home for now. Falcon planned to build her a new house as soon as all the doctors' bills were paid. There were some that both insurances didn't cover, but they didn't mind that, either. Life was too precious to worry about that. Leah thrived in their family environment. She loved cooking for them and being a mother.

Eden was getting ready to go to Baylor, but she was

only going for three days a week and she would drive instead of staying there. She, too, wanted to be close to family. Falcon didn't push her. She was old enough to make her own decisions. He and Leah tried to support her and guide her in the right direction. And Eden was planning on barrel racing again. She'd let that go while her mother was sick.

Dr. Morris kept a close eye on Leah and assured them the tumor was gone and there was no malignancy. She shouldn't have any more complications. They still had to make trips to Houston to see the doctors and when they did, they stayed at the house and visited with the Thornwalls and Alma.

Their happiness had come with a battle, but they'd won and they were more aware of that than anyone. Every day was a blessing at their house. The years he'd been without Leah seemed like a distant memory. She filled every waking moment of his life and most of his dreams. When a Rebel loved, he loved forever.

Leah glanced up and saw him. She came to him and wrapped her arms around his waist, resting her head on his chest. "Good morning, handsome."

He held her, kissing the side of her face. He never got tired of that. "Mornin', beautiful."

"We're fixing you a big breakfast, Dad," Eden said. "Pancakes and everything. Snickerdoodle is supervising." She gently tickled her brother's tummy and he wiggled around, flailing his arms.

John's face split into a big toothless grin. The baby was thriving just like his mother, gaining weight and soon he would catch up to other babies his age. He had the constitution of his parents: he would survive.

A knock at the front door sounded at the same time that one at the back door did.

"Company," Eden said and ran to the front door to let her grandmother in, and then she dashed to the back door to greet Grandpa.

Grandpa rolled an old red wooden wagon into the kitchen. It was bright red now and it was clear Grandpa had redone it.

"Grandpa fixed up the old wagon," Eden said.

"I can remember when Kate pulled you in that thing," Grandpa added. "But not for long 'cause Quincy made an appearance real soon and you were trying to pull him in it. Thought the little guy could play with it when he's older."

"That was so sweet, Grandpa. Thank you." Leah hugged his grandfather.

His mother strolled over and wrapped an arm around Leah's shoulder. "It's so good to have y'all home and happy. It makes me want to tear up."

"We're happy, Kate. Really happy."

"After all the bad stuff, I don't know of anyone who deserves it more."

After breakfast, John went down for a nap and they snuck away for a few minutes while his mother stayed with Eden to help with the baby. Eden had taken the same classes at the hospital as they had to care for preemies and she was very good with her brother.

Arm in arm they walked to the barn. He saddled Titan and swung into the saddle. Reaching down, he caught Leah's hand and pulled her up behind him. She wrapped her arms around his waist and they were off to enjoy a Sunday morning.

They rode to Yaupon Creek. Leah slid from the saddle

and ran to the water's edge. She kicked off her sneakers, stepped in and splashed around. Sitting on the grass, Falcon watched her and thought she never looked more beautiful.

Holding out her arms with her face to the sun, she turned round and round and sang, "I'm happy, happy, happy!" Then she ran to him and sank onto his lap.

He kissed her forehead. "I used to dream of you coming back and wondered what I'd say to you. I never dreamed so much drama would happen or that I would be just as in love with you as I was back then."

"The moment I saw you that day in the park I knew I still loved you."

He undid a button on her top. "Beautiful lady, all we have to do now is love and enjoy the two kids that we have. But most of all we're going to enjoy each other."

"Eden was conceived here on this spot," she murmured.

"Two teenagers without a clue."

"But we knew we loved each other. We just didn't know what to do with all that love. All that emotion."

"Mmm. I was so afraid when you woke up you wouldn't remember that you'd loved me."

"And I was afraid you'd never forgive me."

He looked into her eyes. "Love is like a blooming flower. It has to be watered and cared for to survive. Let's don't ever forget that again."

Her hand slipped inside his shirt and desire awoke inside him like it always did when she touched him. "I will love you forever and remember every moment we have together and be grateful."

He gently took her lips and pushed her down onto the grass. "I love you."

Love was a hard thing to explain, but Falcon knew he and Leah had it and they would cherish it for the rest of their lives. It had gotten them through the heartache and pain. Now the future was theirs.

* * * * *

Love the Rebel family?
Watch for the next book in
Linda Warren's TEXAS REBELS *miniseries,*
TEXAS REBELS: QUINCY,
coming December 2015 only from
Harlequin American Romance!

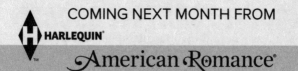

REQUEST YOUR FREE BOOKS!
2 FREE NOVELS PLUS 2 FREE GIFTS!

HARLEQUIN®

American Romance®

LOVE, HOME & HAPPINESS

YES! Please send me 2 FREE Harlequin® American Romance® novels and my 2 FREE gifts (gifts are worth about $10). After receiving them, if I don't wish to receive any more books, I can return the shipping statement marked "cancel." If I don't cancel, I will receive 4 brand-new novels every month and be billed just $4.74 per book in the U.S. or $5.49 per book in Canada. That's a savings of at least 12% off the cover price! It's quite a bargain! Shipping and handling is just 50¢ per book in the U.S. and 75¢ per book in Canada.* I understand that accepting the 2 free books and gifts places me under no obligation to buy anything. I can always return a shipment and cancel at any time. Even if I never buy another book, the two free books and gifts are mine to keep forever.

154/354 HDN GHZZ

Name _____ (PLEASE PRINT) _____

Address _____ Apt. # _____

City _____ State/Prov. _____ Zip/Postal Code _____

Signature (if under 18, a parent or guardian must sign)

Mail to the **Reader Service:**
IN U.S.A.: P.O. Box 1867, Buffalo, NY 14240-1867
IN CANADA: P.O. Box 609, Fort Erie, Ontario L2A 5X3

Want to try two free books from another line?
Call 1-800-873-8635 or visit www.ReaderService.com.

* Terms and prices subject to change without notice. Prices do not include applicable taxes. Sales tax applicable in N.Y. Canadian residents will be charged applicable taxes. Offer not valid in Quebec. This offer is limited to one order per household. Not valid for current subscribers to Harlequin American Romance books. All orders subject to credit approval. Credit or debit balances in a customer's account(s) may be offset by any other outstanding balance owed by or to the customer. Please allow 4 to 6 weeks for delivery. Offer available while quantities last.

Your Privacy—The Reader Service is committed to protecting your privacy. Our Privacy Policy is available online at www.ReaderService.com or upon request from the Reader Service.

We make a portion of our mailing list available to reputable third parties that offer products we believe may interest you. If you prefer that we not exchange your name with third parties, or if you wish to clarify or modify your communication preferences, please visit us at www.ReaderService.com/consumerschoice or write to us at Reader Service Preference Service, P.O. Box 9062, Buffalo, NY 14240-9062. Include your complete name and address.

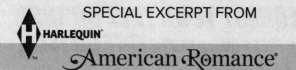
The usual idealism shining in her pretty brown eyes, Violet turned to Gavin, frowned and said, "Obviously we can't adopt baby Ava together." She walked back outside and he followed her. "We barely know each other."

Barely?

While it was true they hadn't hung out together as kids and had run in different social circles—it was certainly different now that they were both physicians.

Irked to find her so quick to discount the time they *had* spent together, Gavin stepped in once again to lend a hand unpacking the trailer, pointing out, "We've worked together for the past five years while we completed our residencies and fellowship training."

"You know what I mean. Yes, I know your preferred ways of dealing with certain medical situations, just as you surely know mine. But when it comes to the intricate personal details of your life, I don't know you any better than I know the rest of the staff at the hospital." Violet plucked a lamp base out of the pile of belongings, rooting around until she found the shade. "And you don't really know me at all, either."

Gavin's jaw tightened. Oh, he knew her, all right. Maybe better than she thought.

For instance he knew her preferred coffee was a skinny vanilla latte. And that she loved enchiladas above all else—to the point she'd sampled all twenty-five types from the local Tex-Mex restaurant.

He tore his gaze from the barest hint of cleavage in the V of her T-shirt and concentrated instead on the dismayed hint of color sweeping her delicate cheeks.

"And whose fault is that?" he inquired.

"Mine, obviously," she said with a temperamental lift of her finely arched brow, "since I prefer to keep a firewall between my professional and private lives."

More like a nuclear shield, he thought grimly.

Don't miss
LONE STAR BABY
by Cathy Gillen Thacker,
available September 2015 everywhere
Harlequin® American Romance®
books and ebooks are sold.

www.Harlequin.com

THE WORLD IS BETTER WITH

Romance

Harlequin has everything from contemporary, passionate and heartwarming to suspenseful and inspirational stories.

Whatever your mood, we have a romance just for you!